AF522670

I Will Ever Remember Them

Anandiben Patel

I Will Ever Remember Them

Anandiben Patel

Publisher • **PRABHAT PRAKASHAN PVT. LTD.**
4/19 Asaf Ali Road,
New Delhi-110002 (INDIA)
prabhatbooks@gmail.com

Edition • First, 2021
Translator • Shri Vadibhai Joshi
Price • Rupees Six Hundred only
Printer • Graphic World, New Delhi

I WILL EVER REMEMBER THEM *by* Anandiben Patel
ISBN 978-93-5322-860-6 ₹ 600.00

Dedicated to

Late Shri Jethabhai Patel
Father

Late Smt. Menaben Patel
Mother

Late Smt. Saritaben Patel
Sister

In my journey from a small village to the paramount post in the state as the Chief Minister the things I learnt, and the inspirations I acquired are the basis and ideals of my life. I am compiling some incidents and occasions in the form of a book, hoping that such incidents will provide you all with new energy, inspirations and efforts to nurture the values in life.

I dedicate the book containing the incidents, proudly to my parents and my elder sister.

My father, Late Shri Jethabhai and mother, Smt. Menaben were very keen in the matter of girls' education even 70 years ago. I fear where I would have been if they had not cared for my education at that stage. At that time in our social set up, the situation was so serious that it was destructive and it was disturbing the social and economic status of thousands of families, who were victims of wrong traditions like child marriage, after rituals, and the barriers between the castes. My parents taught me to fight against the wrong, unfair and unjustified systems prevailing in the society. Father was a staunch follower of the Gandhian ideology. Mother lived literally like his shadow. Without being nurtured with their value-based commitment and culture, I could not dream about my today's position. Saritaben, my elder sister, who was like a mother figure for me, took over the task of educating us. She took a vow to fulfill the dream of my parents and toiled to educate us. She became widow at a very early age and took up the job of a teacher. Due to her contribution and the devotion for our higher education, she always adorns the place of a pious mother for us. During the tough time in my personal, social and public life, her guidance and heart warming support made me stronger to face the challenges. Saritaben played a very pivotal role in my entire life. In reality, my success, my education, culture, self-esteem and the courage were developed under her guidance. I proudly express my gratitude while I dedicate this book to my elder sister, Saritaben.

—Anandiben Patel

Miracles through Minor Tips

The incidence is of 63 years ago. I was in the first standard. Our Maths teacher was explaining the class about the equation 2 + 2 = 4. Suddenly, one boy sitting beside me stood up, raising his hand, he straightaway asked the teacher, "Sir, why 2 + 2 makes 4, and not, 3 or 5?" Entire class was eager to hear the answer, and the teacher replied, "Listen carefully boys and girls; when you will grow up, you will have to visit the market for shopping. You will do the transactions where you will either make payment or receive money from others. It is 2 + 2 = 4, just because, while making payment, you may not give 2 + 2 = 3 and while receiving, you should not accept 2 + 2 = 5. Therefore, 2 + 2 = 4 is the base of knowledge, while the culture lies in rejecting the equation either as 2 + 2 = 3 or 2 + 2 = 5.

I still remember this model reply from our master and with deep regret I say that now the system of acquiring education is, no doubt, widened, but the culture and ideals are absent or have disappeared. The result is obvious. We find that the standard of culture and qualities is still left alive in people having less literacy or those who are uneducated but such virtues are hardly present in the so-called civilians with higher education.

Under such a tragic situation when we come across, hear and observe the real life instances of persons, either of teachers or the other educated ones, our eyes remain open with wide exclamation and we feel in mind a hope that 'yes, still a lot is left and there are people to save all the goodness'.

When I got an opportunity to read the life incidents of mother hearted Smt. Anandiben Patel who was at the helm of affairs in Gujarat as its Chief Minister, I was just overwhelmed with astonishment and joy. Her readiness to help the helpless, her wriggle to fill in a second wind into the discouraged, her capacity to punish the evil, her nobleness to honour the gentle, her eagerness to uphold value appreciation over value depreciation, her grandeur of giving support to the one asking for it, her sensitivity to befriend the unknown, all these virtues if they do not allow our hearts to get submerged into astonishment, then what a big surprise it is! If it was the position of the Education Minister or the Chief Minister, or if there was none but her motherly heart which, by making her a subject in all these episodes, has really provided an awesome height to her life.

Being a *Saint,* while wishing her all good, I would just say, "the position in which you are placed, can do wonders. Whatsoever wonders you are going to create, let one wonder at least be created that in the present day Education System, a lot of talk about career-making is there but that of character-building is hardly there.....let this be done now. You must give priority to the task in our Education System and the race today in our Society of mixing lemon drops of luxury-addiction and worldly pleasures with the life elixir of the young generation must be controlled, and in lemon's place, there should be a race for mixing sugar or the curd of *Satsang-Sadgranth;* you must create such an atmosphere.

The last thing, the willpower of the *Saints,* if mixed with the initiative of implementation by the power of the rulers, then there can be a turnaround of the country. I pray to the Almighty to enable you to do this turnaround. With these blessings:

—Ratnasundersuri

Date: 14-5-2015

Foreword

My life has been formed by innumerable experiences. I was not used to writing, but I was through many such incidents as I felt I must jot down these events. And then I just wrote down the anecdotes and informed quite a large number of my friends about it. They all liked the texts. When I was through them again, I also was overjoyed. Overjoyed not because I was becoming a writer or an author, but because I felt that many people may get inspired by those incidents. All these are true stories, only the names of persons have been changed. These words are not words alone, but a document of my affinity. It is a butter-mix of my experiences. It's only a beginning.

I travel a lot. I meet many people. In the eyes of an uncountable number of teachers and *karmamyogis,* I saw glow of a different kind. I took their advice seriously. I could hear a throbbing consciousness all around. The life stories of some people make me cry whereas the courage and hard work of some teacher or a worker make me and my colleagues feel proud of them. The success of these people struggling incessantly has filled my soul with inner delight. I myself have done a lot of introspection while undergoing these experiences. These experiences have played a major role in my life building process.

I would like to say one thing, I like the books authored by Sudha Murti which describe such type of incidences and contexts. I have had many experiences in the past too. In my public life, the kind of courage and deep understanding which I have observed among the teachers, students and the social workers, the same type of experience and awareness about the stories of hardship to one individual or a group of people are again being experienced by me, first as a Chief Minister and now as a Governor.

Various aspects of the life keep on shaking my conscious. I pray to *Maa Saraswati* to bless me with the energy and capacity to write such experiences and life incidences and express them after compilation.

Dear Readers, I would welcome your suggestions.

Lastly, I express my heartfelt gratitude to a myriad number of teachers and to dear children who are just dreaming about a New World to come up for them.

—Anandiben Patel
Governor
Uttar Pradesh and Madhya Pradesh

Contents

So You Get Fragrance from Gold

A timely solution may be obtained for many of the problems originating in the education system, if the teachers are aware of the information about their pupil. Just as in what circumstances does he study, what type of family base he possesses and what is the economic status of parents of the student. An experienced teacher knows all this but a new one can learn it by experience. So, sometimes, to handle the entire problem in depth, it becomes too late to put the situation in order. The delay causes critical effects on the tender lives of the children. It is, therefore, necessary to exercise proper and prudent care before the circumstances leave adverse effects on their tender minds. Our efforts may meet the success even by learning the things from the rich experience of others. It must be noted that even the slightest reluctance, lack of sensitiveness and improper handling of the situations, may unknowingly implant the evil effects on the students. Therefore, a teacher has to remain aware at all times.

The real task of the teacher is to impart education to students, after understanding each student properly and perfectly.

Today, I recollect an incident which reveals a touching story about an innocent confession of her mistake by a lady teacher, wherein I found that, after her repentance and acceptance, the change in her teaching style was amazing.

The incident occurred during the period of launching the Anupam School project in Banaskantha and Mehsana Districts of Gujarat. For the project, some 15 points were decided to create an Ideal Model School, having qualitative education under public-private partnership. The project got started accordingly. A function was held for awarding the schools having a fairly good performance. Inspirational awards were to be given under my chairmanship. The function was well arranged at the school in the village. A full-fledged programme in the presence of people of the village and academicians of the area was planned out. Their thrust for education and anxiety was overwhelming in the village to welcome their Education Minister. A nice and neat stage and a well-designed dais was ready. Academic cadres along with the educated people of the village and of the surrounding areas were enthusiastic to represent their problems and put their suggestion before me. The parents were eager to adorn the function. The entire village was in the mood of mass celebration. It was just like an ocean of mass participation grooming on the school ground of Fatehpura village in Vijapur Taluka of the Mehsana district.

The programme was specifically for promoting mass awareness among the people and the schools. Improvement in qualitative education was the move planned by our Government. The plea of public and private partnership in the educational field was about to show its impact. At a small village, on the small school, the presence of more than 1000 teachers was a unique event. They all have fared well in their school during the year. They all were praised for their performance. For inspiring them further and projecting their performance in public, the award ceremony at Fatehpura was like a fair place that day.

It is generally observed and we all believe that at any ministerial function, except the dignitaries, no one else can have a chance to speak from the dais, but here the situation was entirely different. It was a shared dais. The awardee teachers were invited to speak freely about their experience, performance and about the response from the people. It was just an open debate in a fresh environment.

From very far off places of the district, teachers had arrived here. Their joy and zeal for expressing their experience and performance knew no bounds. Their preparations were perfect. The process of presenting their views got started one by one. The teachers narrated their performance clearly. Response from the audience and on the dais was obvious. Then came the turn of one Vidyasahayika named Sonal from a Tiny School of a remote village Vav of the Banaskantha district. She had just joined the school. In her job, she had just completed two years. She started her speech. Her appearance was simple but her words were impressive. The audience and we all on the dais listened to her narrating the story in her own words.

"Just before two years, I joined the school as Vidyasahayika. Full of joy and zeal towards work, I presented my letter of order to the Principal of the school. He assigned me the job to take class for fifth standard from the next day. Next day, it was my first practical presence before the pupils of fifth standard. I entered the class keeping two chalk-sticks and an attendance register in my hands. I started calling the Roll numbers—"number one? and the response was "Yes Madam". Continuing the process of taking attendance, the counting reached non-stop, up to number twenty one, but for number twenty two, there was no response. Nobody recited 'yes sister' and I looked up towards the class. A pin-drop silence prevailed. I found that the student having role call no. twenty two was not present. After noting down the name, the class-work was started.

After one-and-a-half hour, at about 12 to 12.30, one little girl came hurriedly running, breathing fast and bewildered, appearing at the door of our classroom. Her shabby dress, scattered hair around her neck and a dirty school bag in her hands made me disturbed. I disliked her late-coming and looked at her feet. She was barefooted. She stood just helplessly and uttered, "May I come in, Sister?" I firmly refused saying "No', you should come in time. I dislike such students who do not come regularly and in time. I will never allow such things in my class."

She stopped at the door quietly for a while and started weeping till there was recess. She went home. My first day ended in an unpleasant mood. Again, on the second day, she came late, stood at the door, asking with urge for my permission to get in the class. I again denied her entry in the class. You will not believe it, but things continued repeatedly for the entire week. She comes late, stands at the door, requests for the entry and I deny her entry everyday. Every time she keeps weeping till the time of recess and disappears thereafter.

But, to my surprise, on one fine day, when I was taking the attendance, that girl of roll-call no. twenty two was present in the class in time. After completing the lesson, I called her near me and asked, "Beta, uptill now why you did not come in time?"

She tried to shun my question, and stood just speechless. I thought for a while and asked her again, "Do you want to study or not? Where were you for so many days?" and when I put my hand on her head, her tender voice burst out. She started weeping. Her tiny eyes were full of tears. I asked for water and gave her to drink it. After a while, she calmed down and slowly began to narrate "Madam, my little infant brother is seven months old. He was born blind but due to poverty, my parents have to go for work on the farms. Even I wish to come to school. I cannot. There is nobody to look after the little one, and take care of household work. In the noon, when my mother returns home, only then I can come to school. Everyday I was getting late and was standing before you, requesting to allow me the entry. It was sheer compulsion for me to take care of my blind and sick brother. But yesterday..."

Now her voice was trembling. She could not speak any more and again started to weep. "What happened yesterday?" asking furiously, I took her closer and asked again. "Then how can you come today?" And her reply was tragic. "Madam, my blind brother is now no more! Lord Almighty has snatched him away from us. He went to the other world forever, keeping me free to come at school regularly in time." She burst out heavily. I was stunned to know the real reason for her coming late in the school. A little girl from a poor family was taking care of her blind lnfant brother, and still was trying to attend and learn at the school!

While listening to her facts, I started hating myself. Why I never thought of asking her the reason for her late arrival at school? Why I often scolded her in a ruthless way? Being a teacher, why I never tried to know the real reason? My social responsibility and the duty of a teacher were actually overlooked by me. The humanity in me had just died, the emotions of motherhood had just disappeared from my heart? I thought again and again and deeply disliked myself. I must have asked her, on the very first day, about reason of the late-coming and could have been helpful. Was it not my duty to visit her house and know about the problem? I should have allowed her to attend the class at her convenient time. It is a very tragic incidence of my life which I will and I can never forget. I have hurt her little heart. But from that day, my eyes got opened, my nature was totally changed. I became very kind towards every child and student. I started loving them all from the bottom of my heart, keeping myself ever ready to help the needy students and their family. The elders and respected senior citizens are also helping me in my efforts with the co-operation and well wishes from the villagers. We are putting in our utmost efforts to make our school a model one in the area. By contributing my additional time, I extend my help to such daughters in destitute and need. We have planted about a thousand trees for extending the greenery around our school campus," teacher Sonal then ended her speech. All who were in the audience clapped a lot.

For me and for all others too, who attentively heard the touching speech of Sonalben, it was a matter to awaken the conscious. Particularly, for the teachers, this incidence is very important. Every child coming to the school needs a special care. Teacher must get aware of the social circumstances of each child, and become familiar to the situation being faced by the family of the student.

Incidents like this have opened a new avenue of thinking for the teachers. In the society, here and there, we find innumerable children, who are immensely eager to get educated, even in the midst of miserable situations. But somewhere and somehow due to our apathetic approach and indifferent attitude towards our duty for the society, many such students are left out from learning. We, therefore, while attending to our normal duties, must understand the psychology of the children and the ways of their behaviour and conduct. It is really an odd job to become a teacher with tender heart, but the love towards little ones, and the sensitiveness towards the society can add an aroma to the glittering gold.

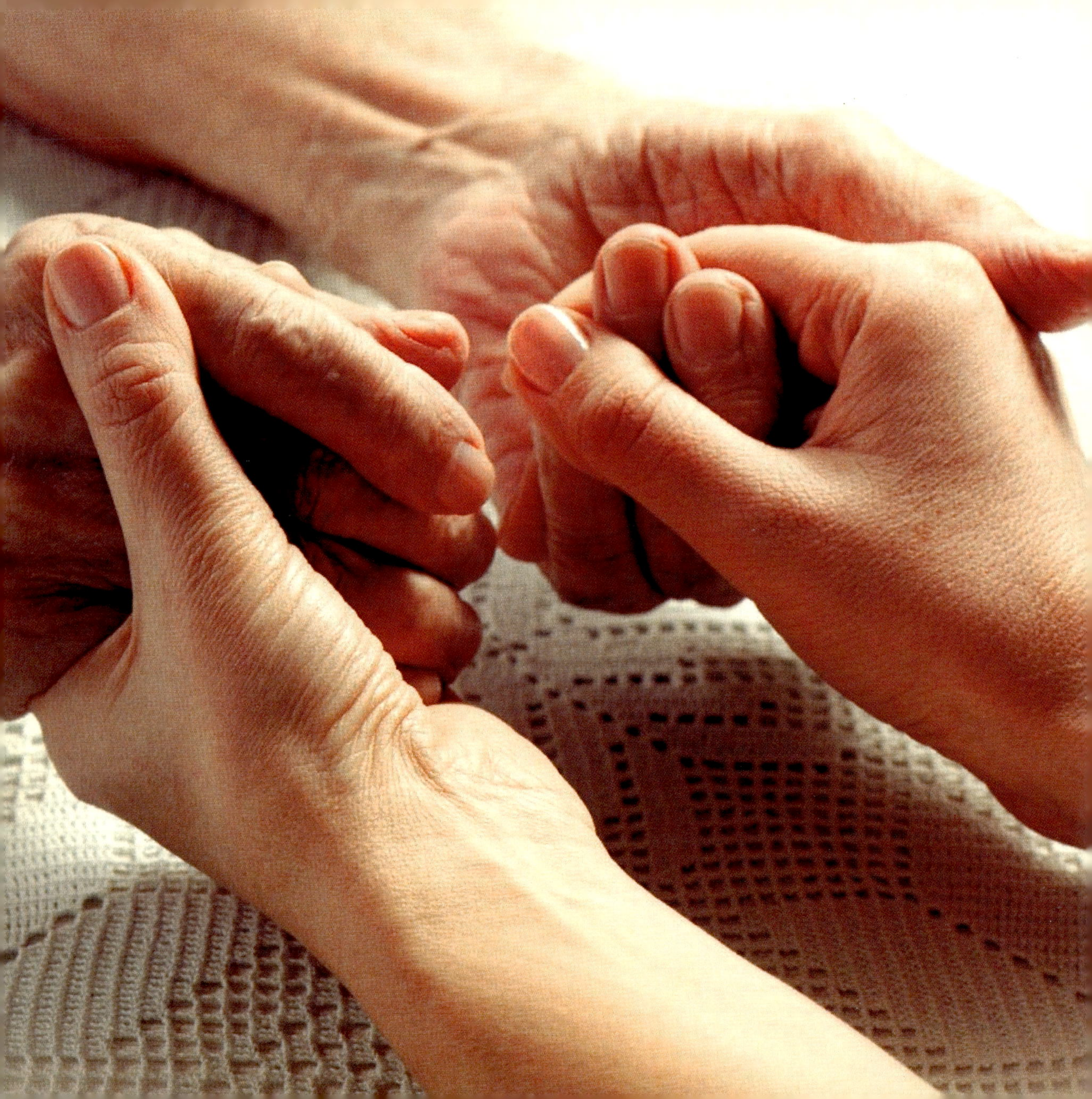

Sympathy is Good, but not at the Cost of Others...

An updated and well-equipped teacher can lead the way to the society. Inefficiency and lack of alertness in a teacher adversely reflects directly on the learning of the students. Problems arise when the pupils are prompt to learn but the teacher makes the job tedious. Normally, the students seldom file complaints for their teachers. Prosperous parents arrange alternatively for educating their children through tuitions elsewhere, but the poor are helpless. They do not dare even to complain for incompetency of the teachers. Sometimes the problems faced by the teachers may be genuine, but in the consequences, victimising the students is unfair and intolerable.

I recall an incident which took place during my visit to Junagadh district. I was just returning from the tour. At night around 10 o'clock, I received a phone call from a public telephone booth. Some two-three students were calling from the other end. They were from a secondary school in the Junagadh District. Over the phone, they complained.

"Madam, second academic session after Diwali vacation has begun at our school, but no arrangement is there to take-up classes for the subject of social studies at the school. What will be our fate during the examination? We are poor students and can't manage private tuitions. You are the only ray of hope and help for us. Madam, just think of our situation when the exam will arrive. Please do something promptly for us." The matter was really serious. Students were serious for study but the teachers did not teach. The question was really serious: "What will happen when our exam is conducted?" The concern was obvious. Some solution must be sought out. I became more curious to hear about their problem and their eagerness to involve me in its solution. I was also happy to know about their dedication towards the study.

I obtained the necessary details from them about their school, Principal's name, etc. and after assuring them for proper arrangement within a week's time, I concluded the discussion telling them to contact me fearlessly as and when required.

I felt that my response was convincing to them, and it was now my responsibility to resolve their problem at the earliest. I immediately telephoned to District Education Officer (DEO). He was attending a marriage function. I, therefore, instructed him to visit that school on the next morning personally, and send me the report after inspecting the matter in detail. Next day, I received a prompt reply from DEO, stating that the complaint of the student was right. A lady teacher for social studies was keeping mentally unwell. She was not able to take the classes for the subject. The trustees and management were sympathetic to her due to their family relationship.

I also felt full sympathy for the teacher, but was firm to issue further immediate instructions in the interest of the students. I was more worried about the important time being wasted. It was necessary that the facilities, for those who want to study, must be extended immediately. Right type of arrangement be made for them.

I, therefore, said, "Let the lady teacher be there in the place, an alternative arrangement to put a good teacher must be made. And see that the syllabus gets completed in the stipulated period of time."

Arrangement at school was put in place and the solution was made but one thing stuck my mind. "How unfair is it? For protecting the job of a teacher, why the future of poor students be compromised? In such situations, timely steps need to be taken. Here in this case, an additional teacher at the school was posted. Students started learning happily. The management of the school should become alert towards such a problem and seek the holistic solution with a broader view, so that injustice to students can be averted in time. It is to be properly understood and practised that power and authority are the means of social service. The constant practice should be put in place for the welfare of the society, the experience of which will give us a joyful satisfaction and complete solution. One should not run away from the responsibility when the good governance counts on him/her.

Don't Ever Express a Doubt Towards a Child, Have Faith in Him/Her

Endless discussions and various ways of deliberations are being carried out across the Nation for our education system. Our civilisation and culture urge for the conduct and ethical values in personality development and character-building. For that reason, the system of education must not be sheer informative but value-based also. It is obvious that in a virtuous society, the doors of development and welfare should get opened in ample numbers. Therefore, an idea and thought was constantly swinging around my mind, that today when I am in a position to do something, I must do it definitely. I believe it firmly that those who are desirous to do something in their life, the Almighty God is always there to help them. He directs us towards new avenues and for innovative actions.

I always feel that our students need to be entrusted some specific task, with love and tenderness, of teaching them the habits of honesty and lessons of loyalty. We should put full faith in their efforts and activities. They may do the assigned work with joy to complete it with due care. They do talk to us if they find the task is tedious. In the school, study material, like pens and pencils, erasers etc. are the daily need for the students. Actions are to be initiated for easy availability of such items. For that job, we should just assign it to a group of students, put faith in them, and observe their accuracy and honesty. Experience their enjoyment and excitement in doing this work. You will find fantastic results of your faith and hope in them. They need your inspiration, encouragement and your faith in their performance.

One day, during a seminar of teachers, I just put forth an idea: "friends, we often express our views that children should become honest and clear in their intentions. But, do we ever assign them the task through which they can practice and prove their prudence, honesty and good intention? Our answer for this is not affirmative. I, therefore, urge to please assign them some responsibilities such as selling of literate wares in the schools, like notebooks, pens, pencils, erasers, sharpeners etc. Let the stock of such material be kept open in the cupboard and in drawers separately, quoting the prices of each item on it. Any student, who needs to buy it, will pick up the thing and put the prescribed price in the box provided for collecting the cost. At the end of each day, a team of students will get the account checked and hand over the collected cash to their teacher.

Friends, the theme Ram dukan–a self sale stall is getting well progressed in many schools.

Specifically at P.T.C. colleges, where the future generation of school teachers is being shaped, the idea of Ram dukan is of immense importance.

Friends, I was surprised and happy to see a Ram dukan at Fatepura school. During my visit to the school, I noticed that in the school corridor, a wooden box was kept. Writing materials like notebooks, pencils, etc. along with erasers, sharpeners and compass boxes were arranged in a classic style. These all were arranged by the students. I was amazed and asked the principal and teachers, "Well done, how is your experience and opinion on Ram dukan?"

All applauded and responded collectively. "There is no loss to Ram dukan. It is a self-managed store. Majority of the children come from labour class and lower society; honesty, sincerity and self-esteem is exemplary in all the students. They all have fully passed in the test of honesty and loyalty. The collection from the sale of materials in Ram dukan, accounted not only exact but showed Rs. 2/- in excess, which shows the well developed honesty in our children."

Friends, here the importance is of trust and faith in students. We should impart in them the sense of responsibility, early in their childhood. Keep them aware and alert towards tiny tasks and teach them the lessons of value-based education. Just the activities like Ram dukan will add the feathers in their crown of commitment towards honesty.

I really became happy with the result and response of this experiment. There are many more aspects through which our students may develop in them the virtues and quality habits.

Please rest assured, the seeds of such developments are already lying in their little minds. You only have to nourish and nurture them. The water of your care, concern and kind attitude will definitely make these values sprouted in them. I always believe that proper education is the deciding step in the direction towards a divine life. Do not doubt them, exhibit your faith in them. Love the students and lead them towards the holistic way of life. Is it not very simple? Can't we do it?

Teachers in the seminar also thought about it. We collectively put the idea into practice. The process started with Ram dukan – a selfsale stall. The theme is getting well progressed in many schools. Specifically at P.T.C. colleges, where the future generation of school teachers is being shaped, the idea of Ram dukan is of immense importance.

"It is easy to bring back an adrift but extremely difficult to exhort a person keeping a wrong perception."

Let the Goddess of Wealth be a Guard of the Goddess of Knowledge

A Daughter is the divine deity in a family. She enlightens two families. Even though her role is multinomial one, yet due importance is not being accorded to her progress. We find that many a times lots of difficulties are faced in educating her. Many poor parents helplessly have no alternative but to keep their daughters uneducated. Their poor economic circumstances are responsible for such a tragic situation. As an unblemished society and part of a prosperous state, can we not think that such girl-child should get good education, enjoy good health and progress well in her life, in her career, and in the overall welfare of the entire society?

Friends, I will like to recall an incident which can inspire us to help the needy girls aspiring for better education. On one morning, a young girl, dressed neatly and simply, came to me at Gandhinagar along with her father. Her appearance was fair but her eyes were full of tears. Looking at me, she could not utter a word but her father said, "Behenji, I am working as a gardener. This is my daughter. She has fared well in 10th standard, with 65% marks." Slowly, the girl also joins her father and starts narrating, "Madam, we are poor people, my father is earning very meagre amount, as a gardner, but my ambition is to study further at Gurukul School. We don't have a pakka house. We dwell in a jhoparpatti and do my study under the nukkad street-light." While she was telling this, I saw her sparkling eyes were full of hopes and lots of ambitions for further study at a better school and become helpful for her family. She again urged "Madam, we don't have means to pay high fees to study at Gurukul School but I want to study there only. We had come to you for your kind help. Will you help us? I want to learn a lot. I will work hard and, along with the study, I will do house-hold work. Please Madam, arrange for my entry at Gurukul." I really was amazed by the way she was talking. Her confidence, her humbleness and self-esteem, while talking, were with presence of full respect and care.

I was just listening to her till she concluded. Now it was my turn to respond. Her absorption in the study and specially, the condition of her poor family made me emotional for helping her. I now felt, "Such a situation is really unfair for society and our system, where the financial hurdles and the monitory crisis become the barriers to the big dream of our poor students."

I then asked for her certificates and necessary documents and also told her to meet me after 3-4 days. She was overjoyed and jumped to express her happiness. On the very second day, I deputed one officer at the Gurukul. After taking a brief from the officer and considering the conditions of the poor family, Swamiji at the Gurukul was kind enough to give a positive response. He admitted her without charging any fees. It was a real kind and exemplary gesture from Swamiji.

It was a matter of joy for me that a poor girl, brought up in the slums, will now learn at a reputed institute like Gurukul. I was rather much happier than the parents of the poor girl. The reason is goddess Saraswati should not be dependent on goddess Laxmi. No society can progress where the wealth dominates the knowledge. We are really proud of our social system and salute the social institutions and the religious trusts that have remained always at forefront to help the noble cause of education.

> "A good rain makes success
> of a farmer's hardwork.
> A good atmosphere makes
> success of a seeker's hardwork."

Humanity is the Highest Religion

वसुधैव कुटुम्बकम् (whole world is one family) is the base on which our social system rests. Entire world is a family. We may not share the happiness of others, but the joy and satisfaction to share the sorrow and grief of others is something unique for us. We get delighted and pleased in being a cause to somebody's solace and help.

Government of Gujarat is keen for health check-up of the students in all its schools in the state. A full-fledged planning is done to complete the task in time. The outcome is obvious if we come to know about the diseases the little students catch very often. We receive advance diagnosis and can arrange for the proper treatment and preventive care. I am happy to say that due guidance and consultation from the specialist doctors is being offered.

In the early morning on that day, I saw a news item in a Local Newspaper, Gandhinagar Samachar. The news was related to a school. I curiously began to read in detail. It was about a girl studying in a local school of Kadi Campus* area of Gandhinagar. The poor girl was suffering from severe diabetes. Even after constant care and medicines, the diabetic counts were not coming down to below 400. Her poor parents were helpless and unable to bear the burden of expenditure for further treatment. The information about the economic status of the poor parent and the seriousness of the disease were really grave and heart-touching for me. It was just a challenge to the humanity, the presentation by the newspaper was so deep and

---

**This campus is situated at 'Gh' Road, Sector-23, Gandhinagar (Gujarat) and here education from K.G. to P.G. and Engineering, Computer Technology & Pharmacy is being imparted for the past several years.*

touching. It created high respect in me, for the editorial and managerial staff of Gandhinagar Samachar.

I immediately acted upon it. Accurate information about the family was sought through the school. The girl was studying in standard 4th at the primary school of Kadi Campus. The poor parents along with their daughter were called at my residence on the second day. Inquiring primarily about the health, hygiene and the treatment taken by her, I contacted Dr. Sujay Mehta, a well-known specialist in homeopathy medicines. Briefing him completely about the case, next day was fixed for the treatment, and accordingly the daughter remained present before the doctor. Her treatment was started in the presence of her parents.

To our surprise and with the grace of God, the diabetes of the daughter is under control now. Within a month's time, the counts have come down to 200 and below. With her continuous treatment, she is gradually getting out of the gloomy situation. I myself find satisfaction as she is being liberated from the serious disease. The parents and the family of the poor girl felt much obliged and overwhelmed with emotions.

"Madam, it is only due to you our daughter has come out from the clutches of death. You just gave her the ray of hope – plus media has really performed its role and duty. The doctor showed the care and kindness towards humanity." I told them, "In reality, I did nothing but tried to direct the way, according to my best intention." Many a times, a proper and timely guidance may give a very big relief to someone, even without much efforts. I want to reiterate that one should not lose any opportunity for people's welfare, because 'there is no religion greater than the Humanity'.

"Even when you come across a right
thing or a good news,
your intellect is not ready to accept it
without casting a doubt over it,
whereas it never readily agrees also to
accept a feeble thing or news, as true."

When will We Realise our Constitutional Commitment?

The aim of education is the holistic progress and all round development of our children. Along with their learning in the schools, they show their talent and competence in extra-curricular activities too. However, some of such talented stars are compelled to stay behind in exhibiting their performance on the field of their excellence. The poor economic condition of their family prevents them to perform. Is it not our duty to promote them and inspire them to go ahead? Yes, luckily there are some industrialists and philanthropists who are keen to carry out their responsibility towards the society. They come forward for financial help. I always felt that with careful and complete co-ordination, the planning can yield us positive and encouraging results.

Friends, I have an incident to share with you. Once I happened to visit a higher secondary public school in Mehsana, a district in North Gujarat. The celebration was for Annual day where the well-talented students were being rewarded with the prizes. Students of all classes from primary, secondary & higher secondary were present at the programme.

Function was also well-attended by the parents to witness the progress of their children. The function started with the prayer by a group of girls from the school. In the beginning of the programme, the girls presented a prayer and also performed a dance. The reports on progress of the school were put before the audience by the principal. Teachers also were equally alert to admire the progress and performance by the students. The other dignitaries on the dais delivered their speeches, inspiring the students, teachers and the management. The process of prize distribution began. Each student one by one stepped up the stage to receive the prize as per the achievement during the year. A little young boy, studying in standard four stood first in the game of chess. His ranking in the game was of national standard. Having remained at first place in chess, naturally the little Lad was looking alert, active and quick in his action. When he stepped on the dais, everyone in the audience applauded him with clappings and cheers. But I heard that his parents were financially very weak. They were unable to bear his further expenses in the game.

I was thinking that a proper training can enlighten the career of such students. When the function was over, and I was just departing, the mother of that student approached me hurriedly and requested for extending some help for her son, with the same feelings, for which I just made up my mind. Responding to her request, I told "O.K. Bahen, I will try for it, please be assured." She left hopefully but the thoughts on chess captured my mind. The game is based on the fundamentals of principles. If one learns it thoroughly and knows how to start the game, very important aspect gets achieved. Your move on the chessboard is dependent on the starting position selected by the player opposite you. The strategy can be learnt only under the able guidance of the experts. In the game, the middle part is also equally important like the beginning, and by learning about the ending or finishing portion of the game, you must achieve the excellence. Without that, you cannot come out of the sieging plan of your opponent and win the game.

Chess-training to children is a good idea. It touched my heart. For offering the best training to that boy, I talked to one or two industrialists for bearing the expenses of his training. The response from them was favourable and the training was started. The boy and his parents were happy. During the course of training, he learnt every aspect of the game with intelligence and developed an expertise in the game.

He was inspired to participate at the state level and he excelled at the National forum. Now the financial help was available to him for taking part in the game at the International level. With his expertise and efforts, and with his mental strength and intelligence in the game, the boy now has earned name and fame in chess. He is now our pride of Gujarat. One industrialist has adopted him and all his expenses for the game are being borne by him.

Friends, for me even today, that reputed player of chess is a little boy who had once appeared on the stage to receive his prize for excellence in chess. I feel 'when we, our society and the system think of such personalities who have been deprived of the bright opportunities, they come out surprising us with their talent. When will our commitment towards the equal right under the constitutional code be realised in toto?'

"However hot the water is,
it extinguishes fire,
howsoover cold petrol is,
it enrages fire."

Faith is a Great Force

Sometimes it is utmost important to understand the incidence in the right perspective. The misleading mania or fascinating fobia, once entered in the mind of a child about the medicine, proves harmful. If a child develops dislike about taking of medicine or injections, it will add to his prejudice towards the prescribed ones. The reluctance to take such medicines results in loss and deterioration of his health. We should not take the matter lightly or casually, but resolve it quickly.

Friends, I remember one such incident which took place during my hospitalisation for heart problem.

It was the year of 2005. I had to stay at the hospital for 4 days. Some children who were to be operated at the cost of government were also accommodated at the same floor of the hospital where my treatment was on. A scheme by our Government was under implementation for better health of the children. I knew that children at this hospital also were being treated under the scheme. Taking the benefit of an opportunity to meet those children, I went to see them. I shared with them the fruits etc. brought for me and used to inquire and ask about their health and well-being from their parents and family. They asked about my health also.

My room at the hospital was well-guarded under police protection. No one without the permission from police can enter the room.

An incident took place. One day, one police man entered my room and asked, "Excuse me, Madam! One small boy wants to see you. May I allow him to come in? I nodded affirmatively, and the boy entered my room in a hesitant manner with a shy look.

"Yes my son, don't be afraid. Tell me what you want to tell." But he could not and still kept on hesitating. I then rather changed my style of asking him so that he would feel free to talk. I asked, "In which class do you study? "In standard six, Mam."

"Very good my boy! But why did you come here in the hospital?"

"For operation! to undergo a surgery, Madam."

"That's good, you will be O.K. after the operation. You will learn a lot and advance well in your studies. You will become a big man. See, I also had an operation."

He now felt friendly with me and started talking.

"But Madam! I am much afraid of Dr. Ketan. I do not like to be operated by him. Let any other doctor do my surgery. Please Madam, do something for me."

I was really surprised to hear all this from the mouth of this little boy. Dr. Ketan, in fact, was the best surgeon at the hospital and was well-known for his skill of surgery. In a counseling tone, I said to the child. "Oh no my boy! You are mistaken. In fact, Dr. Ketan is a nice doctor. Every patient likes to get operated by Dr. Ketan. Don't be afraid!" But the boy was not ready to hear me. He again argued, "I am afraid of him because he gives me injections everyday. Let someone else operate upon me but not Dr. Ketan. Please Madam!"

The boy was terribly afraid. Even he was firm to get well, and convinced to get operated, but his fear for Dr. Ketan was difficult to vanish. I thought for a while, and looked at him.

I could see his request again on his face. His eyes were full of trust in me. He was sure that I would do something for him. With that hope and assurance, he had come to my room.

Considering and keeping the psychology of children in mind, I suggested him an urgent solution, "Look dear, don't be afraid at all. For you, I will arrange another doctor. I will tell this to the authorities of the Hospital. O.K.?"

And the innocent boy was convinced. He now had full faith in me. On the next day, he turned up again and asked, "Madam, did you talk to them? Are they agreeable?" And my words were "Yes my dear, I had already talked to them."

Uttering such unclear words like नरो वा कुंजरो वा, I felt much uneasy and thought of the gravity of grief that might have been experienced by Yudhishthir, the eldest Pandava during the battle of Mahabharata. Luckily, the operation was over. The boy, in fact, was operated by the same doctor, but the child was having much faith in me. Because of my assurance, his fear got disappeared. He did not doubt or know about the fact.

Friends, I felt fully convinced for my false assurance given to him, as it was to become helpful for better health of that child. I went to him after the operation. He was happier than ever because he believed that his operation was done by a doctor other than Dr. Ketan. He told me the same thing and thanked me. I advised him to study well and extended him my best wishes for his future life and good health.

For me, the essence of the event is **'Faith is the foremost factor in life'**. It makes miracles and performs like the nectar.

Auspicious Impact of Devoted Efforts

Many a times, we observe an undoubting and daring nature in children which we seldom find in elders. The programmes and functions of various kinds at the school level help the children in developing their overall personality. Their participation is always joyous for them and their parents. During these moments, their mental concentration and competence are at the peak. They forget or ignore any sort of physical injury. I can never forget the courage and commitment exhibited by children during the days of the devastating earthquake in Gujarat. Their teachers also equally shared the courage and commitment.

Friends, I remember the event rather in a different way.

In the year 2001, on 26th January, I reached Godhara city to unfurl our National Flag. I just entered the Circuit House campus, and was about to sit in the chair. The entire premises began to tremble. My chair got shaky and unset. I realised that it was a severe shock of earthquake. We came down and concluded the ceremony. After the function I visited affected areas and reached home in the evening.

That earthquake, the natural calamity in Gujarat, had heavily affected many of the areas. Thousands of people had lost their lives and thousands of houses and public properties collapsed. Many people were being hospitalised for treatment. The shock was so powerful that the entire public life in major areas of Kutchh and Saurashtra was randomly shaken.

But friends, see the guts of the people in Gujarat, who overcame such a devastating calamity. Without losing the mental balance, people exhibited their firmness, fearlessness and courage.

In the affected areas apart from the hospitals, people were taking shelter at the transit camps. Those injured were being given treatment. I used to visit them and asked about their health and welfare. On the third day of the disaster, I visited a hospital at Palanpur. There I met a little boy. He was resting in the bed and his mother was sitting on the floor near the bed. Introducing myself, I asked the little lad, "How do you feel now? How is the injury? Is it paining? Are you all right Beta?" Listening to my words, the boy looked at me, and his eyes glittered with some unique feelings. Welcoming my arrival, he forgot his entire pains. He got up from the bed and bowed his head in respect for me. Due to the injury on his belly, he could not bend more. He just tried to lift his shirt up from the injured part and showed it while talking.

"Madam, a terrible shock was there when we were on the school ground for unfurling the National Flag. We quickly left our lanes and ran towards the school premises. We all were terrified and tried to take shelter between the Almirahs and the walls. The broken bricks from the upside walls, fell on my head and I fell down on the floor and an iron bark entered my belly."

While listening to him I just thought about the peculiar qualities of his personality. He was not at all uneasy and weakened even in such a state of terrible injuries.

He brings further part of his left-out story. "And Madam, we were to perform a drama. I was to play a role for the Brave Shivaji Maharaj. I was exactly wearing the costumes of the great warrier Shivaji Maharaj. My other classmates were also there to participate in the programme. Madam, it was to be a joyful experience for me. I was to perform the role of Shivaji, for the first time but the cruel shock of earthquake had shaken all our dreams. Having injured severely, when I was brought here, I was just crying and weeping." I thought the boy will break down, but to my surprise, he took a sudden twist in his talk. He, just in a very casual way and in a very innocent mood, moved further to tell his story as if he was trying to inspire me.

"Madam, we have heard much more about you." I simply asked enthusiastically and to enjoyed the expression of innocence on his face.

"Is it so? Good, from whom did you hear? And what is it? Tell me all, please."

"Friends, he started to speak further in a fearless mood. Let us see what he said:

"Madam, the principal of our school attends the training session which you occasionally take. After returning from the training, he would tell us about you and the training. During daily prayer, we listened to him and knew many things about you. We then insisted before our principal, "Sir, please take us all one day to meet Madam Anandiben. We will very much like to see her. Will you take us to her, Sir?" Madam, by the grace of god, you yourself are here to meet me. How lucky I am!"

I left his room. He bowed to my feet with utmost respect. I liked his manner most, not because he admired me, but because of his nature and conduct, which he acquired and adopted through his education. Here I could visualise the fruitfulness of the training class for teachers in a different form. Our Government is very keen to implement many important projects in education. The ultimate effect of it would be that our new generation will get imbibed with an amazing awareness. Real education is always helpful, as a saviour in any adverse situation.

Friends, I must tell you that a little boy in the bed at hospital made me much emotional. His curiosity, and courage, his bravity and simplicity were impressive to me. The tenderness of his talks & his humbleness were strong enough factors to shake me from inside.

Incidents like this leave long-lasting effects in the public life. I just feel satisfied that our Government has constantly kept the efforts alive to improve the qualities in education. The better results of its earnest efforts are just showing up. Devoted efforts only result into such incidences.

The days of Misery are gone, Now come the days of Delight

In our middle-class society, women from the suppressed class and Muslim community have the quest for education. Proper encouragement and inspiration should be extended to them. If we look back at the last ten years, enormous changes are taking place even in the remote areas, specifically where ladies from Muslim community take the lead. I feel much happier to know about the change.

I am talking about the year 2010. It was the Golden Jubilee year of Gujarat state. Kutchh is our border district. Dhordo is a village where the nature has bestowed prime prosperity of white desert. During the winter, the beauty of this Rann area is just to enjoy and imagine. We celebrate 'Rannotsav' in Dhordo which lasts for about a month. Tourists from across the world visit the place during the festival and enjoy the feast of the 'Rann'. I also planned my visit to Dhordo. It was two days' stay for me to enjoy the hospitality and the tradition of welcoming the guests exhibited by the local people of Kutchh. You cannot believe it unless you happen to visit this heaven of hosts, full of humanity.

I was fortunate to reach there along with our nine friends, at about 4 o'clock in the noon. "Welcome-welcome, Madam, how are you?" Miya Husain of village Dhordo greeted warmly. After some casual chitchat, he insisted, "Madam, you please be our guest at my house. My daughters and wife are eagerly waiting for you. They remember you daily. You have been kind enough to provide our village with very good facilities for education. How can we forget the favour you did for us? Madam, we all—including our children remember you." He humbly concluded. I was just overwhelmed with inner feelings and accepted his invitation. "Ok Husain Bhai, we will reach your house after finishing our dinner."

I along with my entire group, went to the residence of Husain Bhai. Their family was staying in a Bhunga, a crafted cottage in classical engineering style. We were surprised by their tradition to receive and treat guests. All members got easily mixed with us, as if I had once visited them in the past also. Remembering the sweet memories, Miya Husain led us towards the ladder of Bhunga, through which we stepped up to enjoy the classic heritage of Kutchh. Bhunga was decorated in an artful way. Our joy knew no bounds, when we saw the creativity, talents and classic settings of the glass pieces in a unique way.

I met Hoorbai—the elder daughter of Miya Husain. In 2003, when I visited Dhordo, she was a small girl of seven and promptly gave answers of several questions asked by me. We saw her unique brilliance. She, with great excitement, showed me the group photos taken by her at that time.

In 2004, Dhordo was just a tiny village. Despite knowing the fact and forgetting about the formalities, I allowed a primary school to function here. The girls from the village had the maiden chance to learn at primary school at their doorsteps. Hoorbai was the first girl to study in that school. She cultivated courage as a girl from Muslim community in the remote and interior area like Banni. Miya Husain was also determined to educate his daughter due to which Hoorbai could fare well in standard 10th—a feat which has never been achieved by any of her family member in the last seven generations! She really ignited the lamp of learning in the area of Banni. Even media published her achievement. At present, a younger sister of Hoorbai is studying in 9th standard. Both the sisters have been given a computer and with its help, they have advanced not only in education but also in their routine activities.

Friends, it was the first time when use of helicopters was introduced in Rannotsav. Locals enjoyed the ride in copter and had the fun to observe their area from the sky. Hoorbai also got the opportunity to sit in the copter for the first time. When she was up above in the sky, the charges of ₹ 2500 to fly did not matter to her. She then told, "Madam, this credit goes to our Prime Minister Shree Narendrabhai who has really made a wonder by transforming the tiny 'Kutchh' in totality. He has developed our area with deep dedication and peer progress. We have now realised that someone is there to care for us. Someone is there to understand our problems and get them redressed without putting us in stress."

Friends, I found my journey very memorable and also a convincing one to my conscious that the areas which remained undeveloped since decades and the people constantly kept ignored and neglected, were now undergoing a change and, the atmosphere is amazing. The tunes in the ambience and air are humming: Happy days are here again.

I was Just Instrumental to It...

Friends, some of our societies are still to come out of their orthodox nature and tradition towards rituals. The female members seem shy of coming out courageously to work. The precedents and customs still remain hurdles for them. Many a times, the faulty customs and usage are incidental in multiplication of their problems.

Since my childhood, my nature is against such unhealthy usages. Addressing the problems of sister women is my topmost priority. Continuing tireless efforts to remove their problems of girls or women is my utmost concern. That's why friends, as and when I get an opportunity, I try to meet them and understand their problems. My earnest efforts are always on to understand women more and more.

In the year 1998, I was contesting the assembly election from Mandal constituency in Ahmedabad district. It is a well-known impression that once the candidates get elected from the constituency, thereafter they never visit the areas from which they represent themselves. They start avoiding the people, neglecting their problems and ignoring the development of the area and welfare of the voters. But my nature is different. I would visit the villages regularly. Very often, on Saturdays and Sundays, my schedule of visits to all the areas of Mondal constituency was regular.

Friends, in Mandal area, a majority of villages have Rajput community as their inhabitants. As per their traditions and customs, women never participate in public meetings. It is their social system which restricts the female members to attend the place or meetings where the males and elderly persons are present. Since I continued my regular visits to such villages, I became familiar with many families. Out of affection and respect for me, gradually the females left their shyness and started to attend my meetings. I changed the system for these women. Casually I would reach among their groups and start talking to them in very simple words. Inquiring about their problems, I was successful in winning their faith. My efforts in convincing them for putting their problems before me fetched some fruitful results.

In the beginning, the task was very tough. They all sat with me but no one took the lead to speak. Just like dumb dolls, all would look at each other. The females of the same age would typically dress in sarees of different colours. I noted it in my mind and took up the point for discussion. Some young girls were also dressed in the sarees of dark colours. I found it somewhat odd and unreasonable. The women in dark sarees were to show that they were actually widows. I really was shocked to hear the dilemma and asked them enthusiastically, "How these young girls, at a young age, have become widows? Have their husbands expired as martyrs or have they died of any disease?" But I received a rather tragic reply from them. "Madam, our community is Kshatriya. The male members get addicted to liquor and wine along with habit of consuming opium. As per the tradition of our community, widow marriages are not allowed. The mortality rate of our male members is higher than usual. Girls at their younger age get married to the addicted young whose life ends early due to the wrong habits and addictions. When our social custom prohibits the young widows to remarry, all such sisters have to pass their remaining life, as widows at their in-laws' house."

I was really taken aback that how the addiction and bad habits ruin the aspiring lives. How the situation becomes unbalanced for the society and the particular community! I would like to tell here that our Government is organising programmes for spreading awareness against such addictions and for preventing use of drugs, wine and liquor. We are ever active to save the younger generation from bad habits. But without social awareness and without removal of unhealthy customs and beliefs, the progress is not possible. We all must think over it.

It was really a critical position for me to bear it. I took a decision on the spot to implement a scheme for helping these young widows by starting schemes like widow-pension. For implementing this scheme, I express lot of thanks to Shri Pragjibhai, Sureshbhai and other workers, who visited the villages and collected the application forms along with documents, proofs and certificates from the eligible women.

But friends, the fight was really tough. The efforts could not take shape unless there was enough co-operation from the administrative wings. The rule was so rigid that the beneficiary women should remain personally present at the office of social securities. It is usually very difficult to change the systems prevailing for decades, but my nature to struggle against the problems came to use many a times. After some arguments and insistence, I successfully explained officials for visiting that village with the active efforts from the Mamlatdar and by the sincere support of our volunteers. We collected about 1,000 applications of the widows from the area, to whom an amount of Rs. 500 per month was made available as widow – pension. One day a function for distributing the cheques to such widows was held and friends, for the first time, I noticed that the feelings of helplessness was absent from the faces of the widows in those villages. I was just happy than ever to bring a smile on those thousand faces. I was just an instrument in it. I saw that the job was petty but of utmost importance. I became just an efficient cause, but to me, the matter of a monthly meagre amount of Rs. 500 to the widows was not important but the initiative towards the liberation from evil customs and usages by a community was a vital one. It was just a little beginning for the widows towards their self-esteem and self-sufficiency. Not only that, the matter was of much importance because its impact for sensitising the system and administration was long-lasting.

ENGLISH
A Apple

And then the Schools became 'Gurukul'

Extra curriculum activity of their choice keep children motivated towards learning. Every child has his own interests. One may like to draw, while another prefers to play. The job of a true teacher is to analyse the likings, attitudes and aptitudes of their students. They must become motivators and guide students to take up proper activities through avenues of education.

Friends, I realised these things on the basis of experience. Why children do not come to school? Just by knowing the reasons you can find out suitable solution. Once we set up our goals and the tasks, we will definitely find ways to achieve them.

It was our Republic Day. After hoisting the National Flag, I entered that village of my constituency for scheduled programme. It was my privilege to honour the students who had participated in the cultural activities. Even on a public holiday, the campus of the school was fully occupied by the children and citizens of the area. The ambience on the ground was humming and the joy of children was at the peak. On the dais, decency and peace prevailed. Turn by turn, each little one stepped up on the stage. I went on hearing their sweet speeches and the inspiring clappings from the audience. It was really a marvellous morning to enjoy their speeches in various languages like Hindi, Gujarati and English too. It was a day of great joy.

This was the same village where only 25 percent of children used to attend the school in the past. The school was just for the namesake. Parents were not bothered and concerned about the education of their children. Inspite of my earnest appeal and repeated requests, no one from the village was listening to my voice. All efforts were futile. The teachers, though enthusiastic, were disappointed due to discouraging attitude of the villagers. The situation was really grave but rays of hope are always there behind the dark.

Three newly recruited teachers were posted to the school. They all were young, enthusiastic and full of zeal and energy, looked well-aware of their duties and knew the importance of education for their students. They took up the task.

Friends, the ultimate aim of changes in education system is to make it an impressive one. The initiatives introduced by the government in the system will ensure that the learner becomes more expert in such subject. Now the question is: "What should be done to make the learning more interesting? How may education be more friendly for its followers – the students?

Friends, let us come back to the school.

The new teachers took over the charge of the situation. Attendance of children in the school was meagre. Young teachers thought: The task is tough. Let us take a round of the village. We will meet the children in every nook and corner of the village. We will inquire about what they do during the day. A child is a kind of creature who never sits tight in the corner.

They observed the activities of the children in the village throughout the day. Some of the boys were playing in the ground by the village pond; an idea sparked in their mind: Let us become their friends and participate with them in their game. This is the only way to win their faith and confidence. We will take up such subjects in which they are interested.

And friends, look at the miracles of the young minds. Next day those three teachers reached the ground near the pond with bats and balls in their hands. It was now the turn of those boys to be surprised. They did not know that the three young folks were teachers in the school. The boys became excited to know that the unknown cricketers will now play cricket with them. In the next few moments, two teams were formed and an exciting and entertaining game began. The boys enjoyed the play more in the company of these new good players. The game continued for two-three days, and thereafter timings of the game were changed. The children were now well mixed with the new players and agreed to play in the evening. It was also decided to arrange matches on Saturdays and Sundays. Everything went well. After some time, the venue of the game was shifted to the school ground as it was big and sufficient enough to accommodate many spectators.

The children were happy now. Teachers allowed them to play the game in the morning and thereafter convinced them to sit in the class for learning. The theme 'Learn while you play and play while you learn' became the best media for the educational progress of the children. Gradually the villagers started understanding the importance of education for their children. The young teachers started getting good respect and better co-operation from the parents. They extended their hands to construct a new compound-wall for the school. Tree plantation and gardening for greenery in the campus also started. People and parents in the village started to play a pivotal role in the progress of the school and the children. A better bonding was established between the village and the school.

In the village, the Republic Day was celebrated in its real sense. Everyone in the village joined the celebrations joyfully. I got the opportunity of honouring three teachers performing their duties with utmost sincerity with shawl and *shrifal*. The students became very happy and people of the village were satisfied with the holistic change in the system of education. Teachers with such calibre can play exemplary role for others to follow. To eliminate illiteracy, the lamp of learning should remain ever enlightened. But the foremost condition is: The teacher must mix up with the children; and the school will definitely turn into a 'Gurukul'. It is essential to keep in mind the future of the coming generations and for that, the 'Yajna of Education' must be kept alight in every nook and corner of the country.

A Son May Go Astray, but a Mother can never Be a Bad Mother

The social system in today's time is becoming complex. Parents have to stay alone and away from their children due to the problems relating to their professions and jobs. There is no need to establish the **home for aged** if proper care of the aged parents is taken by their young offspring. But, how many children do that in the present time? It is only the parents who are all the time worried about their children who are away from them.

Therefore, Saint Punit Maharaj has rightly observed, "Even when you forget the world, never ever forget your parents. During a decade's tenure as an Education Minister in the State, I passed through various events, incidents and experiences where I realised various sentiments of human psychology on hopes, desperation, grief and joy. I came across an incident filled with sorrow and tragedy which is too hard to forget.

At village Shihi of Unjha Taluka in Mehsana district, there lived an elderly person around 70 years of age. He, holding a walking stick, arrived at my office. I was just surprised and thought, 'What purpose had this gentleman to visit me? What work he did have in this office?' I then asked him, "Uncle, from where are you coming and what work you expect from this office?"

"Madam, we, husband and wife, an old couple stay, at Shihi: There is nobody to look after us. We both are now unable to do our routine work. Our only son has to stay in Kutchh for job. The daughter-in-law also has a job, and both of them stay away from us. Our old age and sickness are hurdles for us. It will be a big favour for us if they both get transfered to our village. We expect your favour in our old age."

As the situation was very sensitive and the matter was emotional, I asked him instinctively. "Uncle, are you sure your son and daughter-in-law will really take care of you. If I transfer them to your village?"

"Why not Bahenji, we are very sure of their love and affection for us. We are confident that we will receive their care and concern if they are with us. In the day time, both will attend the school and for the rest of time, we will have their company at our home."

And friends, see the fun of their fate and fortune. I arranged for the transfer of the teacher-couple to Shihi village. Some three months were over. To my wonder, the same old man, a stick in his hand, was coming at my office. I thought he might have come to express his thanks for the transfers. I welcomed the uncle and asked, "Uncle, are you well? How you happened to come here? Do your son and his wife take proper care of you both?"

Friends, I found a shadow of deep sorrow on his face, looking at me helplessly for a while and then he replied in a very low voice. "Bahenji, your concern proved very right. They stayed together with us for 15 days and thereafter left us to stay in a separate house in the village. We both are now victims of their reluctance, and disrespect. Who is mother? and who is father? As their selfish motive has been over, our situation is as bad as before. In addition, we have to hear the taunts from the fellow villagers, which has disturbed us mentally even more. My faith is fully lost. I am here to tell you that my trust on my son and daughter-in-law was false. Madam, I have really been proved wrong." His words of grief made me uneasy. Such incidents in the society are the causes of agony and anger. However, it was his personal problem, and without referring to it in between, I only asked.

"Uncle, if it is so I may issue orders for their transfer back to Kutchh?"

And friends, without waiting for a moment, uncle responded quickly, "No, No, Madam, don't do it, let both be happy here. We will manage ourselves for us. God will give us the strength to survive without them." He took his stick firmly in his hand and without any expectation, he stepped out from my office.

This is why we say "Parents are paramount, even when the child makes mistake. The love and affection for the children keep their feelings firm even after they break the hearts of their parents. Parents remain ever pleased to forgive their children. In their wounded heart and with the injured emotions, the feelings were alive. For the parents, in the advancing age, when nobody is there to take care and support them it is hard to imagine how their hearts may be crying in such a state of helplessness?" Does our so-called civilised society seem to be serious, sympathetic and sincere about such routine incidents taking place everywhere? My reply is 'No!' As in the western culture, **the home for aged** is the alternative and option, but for us one should not forget our parents, leaving all other matters of this material world aside!

Such Incidents are Shameful for the Society

The time has changed, the situations are becoming different. It has become inevitable to leave the native place and stay far away for the purpose of education, job or profession. However, now we all are getting accustomed to it but the situations take serious shapes sometimes. When a daughter in the family has to stay away for the job and when any social problem of specific matter takes place, it becomes more complicated, particularly when the place of posting for our daughter is not a familiar one and is faraway. She does not have enough experience to judge the people or she may not have sufficient time to become conversant to the situation. Under such a situation, the innocent daughter easily gets attracted and leans towards any stranger who happens to help her or provides minor support. And when the person opposite her is not worthy of her, the solution becomes even more difficult.

Please read this incident carefully. One day some eight to ten young men entered my office. They looked disturbed. I noticed that they looked anxious to pour out their anger in a very unique way. The expressions on the face of every person were strong and strange. One young man uttered, "We want to talk to you alone." I then instructed the other people sitting there to move out from the office and allowed the youths to tell their facts.

A young man, with very harsh face and too much anger in his eyes, looked at me. I thought there might be some mistake on my part, so this angry young man had come to quarrel with me.

But the matter was different than what I expected. Let us listen to it. His younger sister had got a job as an assistant teacher in a school at a faraway village.

He, as an elder brother, escorted her to the place of her posting. He happily hired a house for her sister. The parents also stayed with the young daughter for a few days. Thereafter, she used to make up and down to her village during the vacation and on holidays. She was young and unmarried, smart and beautiful. She was very regular to her job and doing her duty religiously in the school.

Friends, incidentally in the nearby locality and just opposite to her school, one family was staying. One handsome but a married person having two children was a member in that family. He was around the age of 25 to 27 years. Daily while going to the school, the young teacher had to pass through the road near that house. Due to daily contact, the married person was becoming helpful to her in some petty work at the school. He used to visit the school. During the course of time, both were attracted to each other. With the passing of time, that school teacher started staying as a kept with that married person. She was still doing her job as before.

Now, the daughter's visits to her parents and the village became fewer. She almost stopped going to her parents and her behaviour towards parents and relatives also changed. This issue was being criticised socially. The verification took place at the place of her posting and the parents got worried to know the real reason. The situation was too tough to digest. The prestige of the parents and relatives was at stake. The shock was unbearable and the incidence was unbelievable to the friends and relatives of the family. They were ashamed to show their face in the society.

I heard the story from the angry brother, and understood the entire situation.

I then asked, "What is to be done now?"

His face was still full of worries for her sister. He just declared his firm appeal to me, "Madam, terminate her immediately from the job. We don't wish her to remain in the job anymore. If you don't do, we are going to take her back to our village forcefully from the school." His anger and worry appeared in every word he uttered.

I tried to explain to them, "Please don't take the law in your hand. Never enter in abuse and absurdity or make any foul action on anybody. Our daughter is not a minor. In case matter goes to court, your efforts will be in vain. Even though your concern is appropriate, the solution of such type of problem cannot be sought by applying force. As you have approached me, I am here to help you, provided you obey my instructions."

But friends, the brother was too firm to agree. He kept on insisting on termination of his sister's job, but after some time, due to my way of explaining, he got convinced gradually. It was true that they all had come to me for help, but for me, it was a matter of the life and the career of a young teacher. After thinking deeply, I suggested them the way, which was easy and also suitable for protecting her interest. I told them, "You just visit the school, as if you are totally unknown of the facts. Just pretend it in a perfect way. Take a vehicle with you. Behave in a manner as if there is someone serious in the family in your village. Under such excuse, you bring the sister to your house, and then try to explain to her the way out from the situation."

Friends, they ultimately got agreed to my suggestion. On the second day when they brought her home as per my advice, I got her termination order cancelled in the morning that was handed over to her in the evening.

Here the question before us is: "How many daughters may be taking such hasty steps in an unwise manner, without thinking about their future? The consequences of such hasty decisions not only made her life miserable but the entire family and the relatives also had to suffer out of sorrow and social criticism. Nobody was happy. How strange is it? Even after acquiring good education, are such incidents in the society not shameful? It is really a matter of serious concern that some solution of even such a situation has to be worked out and something has to be done. Of course, when we have to choose between carrer and life, the option of life is to be chosen.

Education is for Developing the Character, not to Destroy It

Our society and the institution of matrimony are part of our social structure, based on the firm foundation of culture and character. Education adds the force to strengthen them and for that reason, any act of lowering the conduct and character cannot be tolerated when we say we are educated.

In our system of primary education, we appoint education inspectors at district level. Today, I have to narrate a story of one such inspecting officer. In our Mehasana district, an incident came to my knowledge.

A young lady got her job as an education assistant (Vidya Sahayak) in a school. The place of her posting was at a distance of 9-10 kilometers from her native village. The young lady used to commute by a bus, coming regularly to her village. With her utmost sincerity, she used to attend the school and take the classes with joy and zeal. In the evening, she would manage to return home by any available means of transportation. There was a very pleasing atmosphere at the school, and the children were also attending the school cheerfully and attentively. Educational activities at the school were in progress in an excellent and enjoyable way.

The inspecting officer visited the school for its inspection. Here the inspector, instead of carrying out the inspection of the school, started to inspect the lady teacher! This inspector reached the school on his scooter. He would intentionally take a route from where the lady teacher used to come to the school. One day, he was truth in the allegation by the teacher. The conduct, behaviour and the intention of the Inspecting officer were all pointing to his guilt. His act was considered to be criminal, and the elements like him making the entire system dirty, cannot be tolerated. Such elements have to be dealt with sternly and I thought it was my duty to take a harsh step in the case. I ordered for his suspension and further investigation in the matter against him.

"Happening of an event is not in our control, but the way of interpretation of it is always in our hands."

Truth Always Wins

People sometimes hide facts for getting their work done. They don't even hesitate in bringing fake medical certificates from doctors, showing that they suffer from some incurable disease.

But friends, do remember; no one can progress or go ahead in life using false practices. Reality and truth will always appear one day and the structure built on false foundation will ultimately collapse. That's why when a responsible teacher, instead of imparting value-based and qualitative education to the students, adopts untrue tactics, we get hurt from the core of our heart.

Friends, I will tell you my own story. My eldest sister Saritaben devoted her life for our education and care. Today whatever I am, is due to her. She played a very important role in my education and all round progress. She always opposed the lies and fought for truth. She was very intolerant towards the wrong deeds due to which we always abstained from doing one. She trained us since our childhood in cultivating all good habits. She, even today at the age of ninety two, enjoys her life.

I remember an incident when I was the Education Minister of Gujarat. Some people from a village went to see Saritaben. They requested her to convey to me to keep them free from the mess of transfers because their wives are posted here as teachers.

It was a well-known fact that some vices like corruption, enmity etc. have prevailed since long in the matters of teachers' transfers. I took one important decision for changing the process from the grassroot level. To make it transparent, the camp method for transfers was implemented. I specially resolved to consider the cases of transfer, where there were genuine problems due to serious ailments.

During further investigation, it was revealed that their compounder assistant took money and put such remarks on each case paper. They all were caught.

I ultimately apprised Saritaben of the whole story. She was shocked— Can any teacher dare to do this? How shameful is it? These people, who are committed to lead the society on the right way, had shamelessly adopted a way based on untruth and lie. How can we tolerate such things? And, that too for a petty matter of mere transfer? She just said to me, "Your decision seems proper and right."

I then personally called those lady teachers and asked why did they indulge in such unfair act. It was yet another shock when they said, "Madam, we neither bought these certificates nor we know anything about them."

I was puzzled, "Then how come these papers are here in your files? Who put them there?" After discussing some issues randomly, and through minor inquiry, I came to understand that the ugly job was undertaken only by their husbands. They just tried to make the tedious task of transfer easier for their wives.

The teachers were ashamed. They confessed the truth. Telling me, in a request tone, their words were, "Our husbands have done the unfair act but the punishment will befall on us. With kind and humble heart, please forgive us."

Friends, keeping in mind the lessons I learnt from Saritaben during my childhood and in young age, I delivered justice to the erring lady teachers. Without penalising them, I forgave them and warned that the decision on their transfer will be made in the camps as per the process. I said, "But do remember, never resort to such unfair practice in life. Take utmost care in future that no relative or member from your family does such acts. When you are on the seat of authority or power, treat everyone alike." This joy is a supreme one for me, ultimately the truth always wins.

Our Duties as A Citizen

In our society, the widows and divorcees are desirous of becoming self-reliant in their own ways. They need some encouragement. Some efforts from our side for their support are inevitable. It is often observed that members of their own family and relatives put hurdles in their ways to progress. Very often the divorcee women are being harassed by persons from their past, relatives and their ex-in-laws. Such poor ladies are given threats also. Under such circumstances, the courage and firmness by the women make the problems easy to resolve.

Friends, this is an incident from Anand city of central Gujarat. From there a daughter telephoned me: "Madam, I have taken divorce from my husband, he is a cruel fellow. He would go on harassing me almost daily. I have taken transfer to another village to save myself from his harassment. When I return home in my village, the fellow will stand at the bus-station. He will talk absurd and dirty, in awkward words." The phone call was about to be over when I inquired from her about the details. How was the family? And under what circumstance had she to take a divorce?

Friends, for taking my next step, I asked her, "At what time do you leave for job in the morning? And when do you return?" I then assured her and told her, "O.K. Don't worry. I will see that your difficulties will get over soon but don't get depressed. Keep your confidence intact and face the situation with alertness of mind. You will not have any further problems."

I informed the Collector of Anand. All details of the case were updated to him over the phone. If required, the collector may take police help in the matter.

On the second day, some policemen in civil dress were deployed at the place. The lady was still to alight from the bus. The Ex-Husband of that lady reached the place before her, and started abusing her in absurd and dirty words.

The policemen were ready for the action. They asked her while she was alighting at the bus-stand, "Bahen, is this fellow harassing you? Is this the same fellow against whom you had a complaint?" She said, "Yes." Police caught hold of that man immediately and took him to police station. He was strictly warned, "If you will again try to trouble her, take note you will be behind the bars." The fellow was ashamed and went away.

The daughter conveyed me her happiness and thanked me for the quick help. Small incidents like this are a routine in daily social life. A lady when thinking of asking help from Gandhinagar, how severe her problem could be? Nobody helped her in the difficulties she was facing daily. Being helpless and with lost faith in the system of social set-up, she thought of telephoning me at Gandinagar. As a citizen of society and the State, is it not our duty to think about happening of such shameful incidents? Our sympathetic and awakening attitude only becomes helpful to our daughters and sisters.

"Talk later about calming
down desires,
first let us purify them.
The purification
of desires will
essentially lead you
to a healthy mind."

The Unique Features of Indian Civilisation

Many a times some minor problems can be resolved by common sense. Our society is ever eager to honour its responsibility. The need is to lead the way. I had the charge for Women and Child Welfare Department. It, therefore, happens on many occasions to pay visit to women's protection centres (महिला संरक्षण केंद्र).

At Himmatnagar, a new building for women protection centre was ready and I went there to inaugurate. Minister Shri Ramanbhai and Shri Jaysinghji were also present. After the function was over, I was just collecting the details about orphan daughters and mothers staying in the center. I was also inquiring about their needs and requirements. It was informed to me that a girl aged about 14 years was pregnant. I wanted to have more details from the Director of the centre, about proper care for her delivery and nourishment of the newborn. I also talked to the Director for further study of that mother girl. Our talks were on. Meanwhile one lady of 20-25 in age arrived there and told me, "Madam, I have selected a young man for me. He is agreeable to marry me. Her mother is also ready to accept me but our Director is denying permission for my marriage."

I was so happy to hear such innocent words in the form of a complaint from the little loving lady. Her sweet voice was mixed with joy, zeal and hope for her future life. I found her much aware about importance of proper time for her marriage. Immediately I asked for other details and knew about the difference in age between the two. It should not be more than 10 years. In this case, it was not. After considering the proposal in right perspective, I accorded a special permission for her marriage.

Friends, the inaugural function was concluded. We all— The Collector and District Development Officer and Minister Shri Prafulbhai Patel proceeded to the Circuit House. Planning for the marriage of that lady was done under enjoyable and auspicious moments. It was decided that the society will do the preparation for the marriage. Stage decoration and catering arrangement with gift, clothes and **Kanyadan** was managed by us. The only thing remained was to obtain consent from the boy and the girl, that is, bride and bridegroom. That part was to be performed by Shri Prafulbhai.

An auspicious day for wedding was fixed. Invitations got printed. In the auspicious presence of respected people, the marriage was arranged. The Daughter was adorned as a beautiful bride, with the Saubhagya sindoor on her forehead and in her hair. She was very happy with various types of gifts and articles. All necessary items and articles were at their disposal to make their family life a full-fledged sucessful one. The planning was perfect. Even a stove with gas cylinder was handed over to her along with a Time deposit certificate in her name to secure her future, a goodbye to the daughter.

The time to depart had arrived. There was unique joy on everybody's face enjoying the marriage of the daughter, as if she was their own daughter. All types of arrangements were made by the society itself. People were very happily saying, "Please provide us more opportunity to participate in such kind of social work. This is a holy and religious work."

It is a unique speciality in Hindu civilisation to do something helpful for others, to give away generously as more as one can. Each one in the society possesses a sense of sacrificing for others. The need is to lead the way—the process takes a start by proper direction.

"World asks only
What you have?
The Almighty God
just inquires,
"What is it that
accompanies you?"

Any Carelessness by An Officer not to be Tolerated

Our government helps the people in need. It is the most necessary thing that the help should reach such people. Any negligence on the part of administration defeats the very purpose of the help. For everyone in Government machinery, it is the duty towards the society. Duty must be performed with devotion. Lack of devotion is severe loss to the society and the government too. Everyone in the chain of administration should carefully bear this in mind. Each one must perform with sensitivity and dedication towards the society. Please look at an incidence of sheer negligence.

In the State, at district level, **Garib Kalyan Melas** are being organised. Poor, deserving and needy families and their members are being provided with the help either in monetary terms or in the form of materials like utensils, products or machinery, etc. for carrying out their livelihood and expansion of their occupation. This time, Garib Kalyan Mela was held in Banskantha District and at Palanpur city. I was to visit the Mela. It is my habit that at whatever place I go, I carry out the review for the departments which are under my authority. On that night, I suddenly paid a surprise visit to the Nari Suraksha Kendra functioning at Palanpur. I saw six to seven tricycles in a corner of a room. I inquired, "Since when are these cycles lying here?" Reply was: "Madam, at least for the last 2-3 years." I inquired further, "Where is the Director?"

Someone said, "Madam, she does not stay here."

And it was for me to go deep in detail. I verified the facts personally and on the spot. It is my experience that real situations can be understood only if you pay proper attention through personal visit. I also inquired from the Department of Social Welfare. They reported, "All tricycles have been allotted to the beneficiaries. But they did not turn up to collect the cycles." Friends, see the bad part in the story. Nobody in the department concerned has bothered. No one felt the necessity to know why those beneficiaries did not approach. The reason for their not turning up was never known to anybody. In case the reason could have been intimated that the beneficiaries now did not require the help, then the tricycles could have been allotted to other needy people in the area.

In this case, if the responsible officer in administrative wing would have acted with sincerity and in a sensible manner towards his duties, the Government could have been saved from a state of disrepute. The Government makes the schemes for the poor and the needy for making them self-reliant, but due to some scattered negligence by any of the officers in administration, the needy and disabled persons remain deprived of such help from the government. Every officer and employee in the government must be sensitive and dedicated to his work for the welfare of the people. They should keep in mind that the opportunities to serve the people should not go waste.

As Long as Humanity Exists, Acts of Benevolence will Continue

Surat is the silk city of Gujarat. It is also a city of jewel and place of sparkling gems. For various programmes hosted in the city, attendance becomes a must for us. Once, for such a function, I was in Surat. As the night halt was planned in the city, I thought of a visit to Nari Sanrakshan Kendra. In the early morning, suddenly I thought of visiting the campus of the Nari Kendra. Immediate implementation is my habit. I knocked at the gate of the Nari Kendra, early at 8.00 o'clock in the morning. Reply from the Gateman was. "Still it is time to open, come after 10 o'clock."

It was surprising. Why is it so? Why do they not open the gate? Ultimately I had to introduce myself and I asked the gateman to open the gate.

But the sister inside the gate was in puzzle. She was confused and frightful, but she opened the gate. I saw 15-20 children playing inside the premises as soon as I entered the floor. On my going near them and looking at their little hands, I saw the symptoms of scabies on the hands of 2-3 children. Meanwhile, other children came to me one by one to show their hands and fingers. They felt better, their faces were expressing the feelings of assurance that there was someone to listen to and someone to love them. The condition of those little children was really miserable.

On that morning, I felt too bad. I was very unhappy and sad for such a situation. Even though there was a doctor at their help, children had to suffer from such a dirty disease of skin! I waited there till the staff came. I met the sisters and the superintendent. I visited every room and inspected each corner of the premises. There were heaps of dirty bed-sheets and tornout bed rolls in the rooms, old and dirty clothes were lying there in scattered condition. The furniture also was broken and old. No sign of daily cleaning was in sight. At some corners, dust, mud and dirt were accumulated.

With unhappy and grieved heart, I was back at the Circuit House. The matter was very disturbing one. The task is to be taken up on warfront and I took an oath for resolving it. I summoned the officials from Social Welfare Department. I narrated them the entire situation at the Nari Centre. It was the matter of health and hygiene of the children. Treatment was to be given on urgent and priority basis. Skin specialists were called for at the place. Bahen Darshana and other sisters had taken up the task and did the entire planning. It was arranged that doctors would visit the centre regularly and provide treatment of scabies to the children. The old clothes, bed-sheets and bed rolls were destroyed, and burnt and the entire ward was made germ free by applying antiseptics and other medicines. Municipal Corporation, Surat also took urgent steps cleaning the entire premises of the centre, and pesticide sprinkles were arranged to make the premises very clean, neat and septic-free.

All concerned performed their duties with dedication. Today the building is under repair. No sign of any disease is left there. For this institution, I appointed seven ladies who voluntarily work for collecting necessary materials for the children from the society. It comes sometime in my mind, 'Why is it so? Why the officers make mistakes while performing their duties? Are these poor children not from our society? We neglect them only because they are orphans? In these centres, such women get shelter who had been victimised by the society. We must perform our duty towards them, and extend the hand of help to such helpless.'

For this work, I give credit to the society as this important objective is carried out with the help from the society. Humanity still survives in the society. This is an example of it. As long as the humanity survives, such benevolent work will continue.

"Bad habits and addictions not only damage the character, they destroy your delight also."

Where the Society is in Support, Nobody is Orphan There

Today, I will talk about a different aspect of Nari Kendras in Gujarat. They undertake the responsibility of offering shelter and services to the women in distress. Not only that, if time comes, the centres work for such women in helping them to choose their life-partner.

I will like to cite an example. Once I received a letter from Rupaben, Chairperson of Nari Suraksha Kendra, Surat who had sought permission of marriage of two girls staying there. Permission was granted, so Rupaben and her team requested for my presence at the marriage. I happily gave my consent.

It was an ideal deed being carried out in the society. I reached Surat at night to bless the daughters. Very presentable and pleasing preparations were done. Twinkling decorative and colourful lighting-series were arranged. The volunteers were active as if their own daughters were getting married. Varities of gifts and presents were offered. The Corporators of BJP performed the Kanyadan ritual. Collector of Surat was also present. While bidding farewell to the brides, everyone got emotional and was in tears. Both the daughters were happy to have suitable life-partners.

After blessing the brides, I returned home happily. It was a unique atmosphere which got entrenched into my mind. It was a supreme satisfaction in my heart. The society adopted the orphan daughters and they got settled in their family life. I really appreciate Rupaben and her associates for the excellent arrangement. Where there is humanity in the society there is no need for Nari Kendras.

Self Help is the Best Help

I have often visited various social security welfare centres. The aim of women welfare centre is not merely, as I said earlier, 'to take care of women, but they should be protected, they get employment and their life becomes active and self-supported'. As they get shelter in the centre, after passing through very odd situations in their life, they must feel free now to enjoy happiness, peace and sense of self-respect. The objective gets fulfilled if such an atmosphere is maintained at the centres. My struggle in this direction is for attaining that objective.

Friends! I proudly feel that my efforts have not gone in vain.

I remember my visit to a Nari Suraksha Kendra at Godhara in Panchamahal district. The Centre was having a big compound without a single tree. The entire ground was just looking empty and barren. It was possible to grow or plant the trees around the ground. Even some cash-crops could be cultivated. Vegetables could be grown easily as there was fertile soil and plenty of water to cater to the need of vegetables and crops. Having noticed all such suitability, I casually asked the Director of the centre, "Please tell me, what activities they do for the entire day?" The details narrated by her for the routine and daily activities were not inspiring. I thought, 'Why not call them all to know their ideas?' I told the Director' "Please call them all here." They all came, we sat together. I inquired about their health and chatted with them. They were cheerful while expressing their feelings. I then asked them, "How do you pass your entire day?" All became attentive and I immediately put a proposal, "See, here you have very fertile land and plenty of water for irrigation. Why not we grow vegetables like radish, carrot and gourd for you and the children in the centre?"

They all found the idea quite an amazing one. They started talking about it and interestingly, some of them were keen in counting the benefits and profits out of the activities. End of the discussion took on an encouraging note for growing vegetables, trees and some fruits and flowers in the open land of the centre. But the ladies were lame for the work of tilling the ground. The prime problem was to use the plough in time. Non-availability of agricultural tools was yet another hurdle. The solutions were not easy. I was just thinking on it, 'Why not any department in the government be involved and get the job done'. However, the arrangement should be sustainable. And friends, to my surprise, an inspiring voice came from the little gathering there. The fellow was a disabled person but he said with a confidence, "Bahenji, don't worry. Leave it to me, for such a little job, why should you ask for the help from someone else? I have got a tractor of my own. I will plough the plot. I will also make the leveling of the land by the tractor, and will not let my sister to bear any trouble."

I was really overjoyed to see the readiness and his feelings for helping for the noble cause. I accepted his offer and greeted him for his generosity. I also extended him best wishes for the success and support.

For our society, such self-helpers are the real semblences of sacrifice and pride. We can judge their strength on the basis of such an example. One who loves the work, need not have to wander for the help. Our own hands are the strength from God—is the mantra in their vanity.

"Oh, God, if I will commit
the mistake constantly,
please give me the
strength at least for not
repeating the old ones,
often and again."

To the Pure, Everything is Pure

One NGO at Jamnagar was permitted by the State Government to run a centre for women welfare. Once I visited and meticulously inspected it. I entered the kitchen. Two daughters (girls) were making the chapattis. Their style of preparation and designs were the same as we do at home. I also tasted the Daal Rice and vegetables too. Every item was very tasty. I felt proud for them for their neatness, cleanliness and perfection in the kitchen. I saw them enjoying the work assigned to them. Their dedication at duty was exemplary. I initiated the talk with them.

"What did you study?" "We are in M.A." was the reply from both. "What do you plan thereafter?" There was a long pause. I insisted for reply, but both remained quiet and cool. I quickly realised their silent reply. They were looking more puzzled about the way to study further, and decision about the direction of their future. They looked helpless too. I, then obtained a list of girl-students in the class of M.A., B.A. and Standards 12th and 10th but I did not utter a word there at that time.

After reaching Gandhinagar, I called my officers. Obtained such lists from all districts. I found that the girls who completed the study for 10th and 12th were not at all aware about the courses available for them to acquire employment. This is something serious, my friends. Any aspirant who wishes to select the field of his/her choice, must possess the information of that field. It is also imperative that these girls should become self-reliant. Something is to be done. The need was to create the opportunities and arrangement for them to progress further with their own prudence and skill.

Friends, it was a win-win situation for me, as the education department was in my charge at that time. I got it resolved from the Education Department that priority in admission should be accorded for the daughters studying, with the intention to do P.T.C. or B.Ed., so that they might get the job and become self-reliant in their life.

We now see better result of that decision. Many such daughters got the admission, their hopes increased and they started their studies with more joy and better preparation. They got through the examination with better marks and also settled down in their jobs. I felt satisfied by heart. I was much happy as something better was done for the daughters in need. It was really a good visit when I decided to talk to the girls at women's welfare centre at Jamnagar. The idea was the outcome of my visit and its benefits were extended through the scheme implemented at the state level.

Friends, my various visits at varied places, personal interviews, talks and interaction with the masses are the useful tools to decide about the need and welfare of people. The self-assessment about matters affecting interests of the common man and their problems comes to our help, and if these problems are to be resolved in any case, the ways so created make a way for everything (i.e., मन चंगा तो कठौती में गंगा)."

Kudos for Such Youth

Youths are incredible asset for any nation. With their will power, they can become mentor for the masses. They can solve and simplify the social problems easily. The enthusiastic young men and women devote their health, wealth and mind for the upliftment and welfare of the society. They even provide inspiration to others.

Their volunteering and firm resolves take the society to newer heights.

Sometimes, we may doubt, "Whether such things can happen in this age? Whether such stories are possible? But my feeble faith became stronger when I was a witness to one incident of **oath taking** during the public celebration of **Swarnim Gujarat**.

In the year 2010, Gujarat State had completed 50 years of its formation as a new State. Celebration of Swarnim Gujarat was to take place with the will-skill and support of the people of Gujarat. Foundation day of the State was celebrated on 1st May at Amareli—in the auspicious presence of the then Chief Minister Shri Narendra Modi. It was also arranged simultaneously that the Swarnim Yatra Rath will take a round of all big cities and the villages. It was aimed at showing all-round development of Gujarat to the people of the State. People were full of joy and enthusiasm towards the Swarnim Yatra.

The yatra with its Rath decorated and detailing the story of development, was to arrive at Detroj town. Being an in-charge Minister of that area, I was there at the programme. The people were taking the Swarnim oaths, in general, at the programme.

During the public meeting at Detroj, one young man Raju stood up and declaring his oath, he said, "Just give me a telephone call to remove the dead bodies of dogs, cats and pigs who die in your village. I will attend immediately and remove and dispose them off at a distant place, to keep your area clean and free from epidemics."

Friends, I was just listening to it. How courageous and clear desire it was? It was very strange oath particularly for today's youth! I, at that time, felt it this was a causal thinking that this young man might have told this out of his immediate emotions and inspiration.

But friends, my doubt about his oath was wrong. Raju has maintained and fulfilled his oath. He kept himself ever ready to attend such phone calls. He would immediately reach the village where the dead body of animal was lying. And arrange for its disposal. I feel happy that my doubt about him was wrong. I salute that young man Raju of Detroj.

One such oath is taken by another young man. He said, "I have a JCB Machine of my own. I will use it for the service to the society at least for two days in a month, I will not charge for it. Who so ever in the village wants to fill up the ditches and make his land in level and improve the roads by removing 'Babuls', will take the JCB from me. It is my duty to keep our village clean, neat and beautiful.

Normally, any person with commercial mind will think of gain and make calculations in mind. Rental charges for JCB machine per hour cost ₹ 500 to 700, which can add up to ₹ 12 to 15 thousand for a day. In a month, for 2 days his profit or earning will get reduced up to ₹ 25 to 30 thousand. But this young man did not care for such money. For him, the beauty and the cleanliness of his village were of prime importance. Such youths are the real claimants of congratulations and kudos. For the villages, our Government has launched a scheme called Gokulgam. The credit actually goes to so many such youths who are really keen to ensure cleanliness.

We always remember Mahatma Gandhi when the concern counts on cleanliness. Once somebody asked Mahatmaji, "What is your greatest worry?" Bapu replied, "My greatest worry is the reduction of an inclination of service to the society among the educated class." The remarks by Bapu are right in today's atmosphere and such events of oaths in front of us, when taking place, create hopes for any citizen for a successful Launch of Swarnim Gujarat. It is now beyond doubt that, till such assets of the inspiring youths are with us, the dream for Golden Gujarat will soon become a reality.

Why Do We Need to Punish Efficiency?

An employee when performs his assigned task in a committed and devoted manner, he/she gets respect and love from everywhere. Demand for such employees who are always efficient at their work is always there. But from the minds of common people, the questions and doubts never get cleared about numbers of such employees in the Government, who do their job sincerely and systematically. It is also true that the tact, tendency and the way adopted by the officers keep the employees ever active and alert.

It was my surprise visit to the Stamp Duty-office, in Gandhinagar. Such sudden visits are sometimes necessary to know the real and exact situation at the place.

On my visit, I saw that, some of the employees, males and females, were yet to settle in their chairs. Some of the employees reached late and some had already reached, but they did not make record of their attendance in the muster roll.

In the matter of the allotted task, many things were pending. Classification of records of different types of land was yet to be carried out. On the empty tables, heaps of files were piled up. For some unknown reasons, the works remained in pendency. After taking the status of absentees, a note was prepared about the employees not attending or remaining absent regularly.

While inquiring about all such matters and activities, I happened to enter a room where the process of index and calculation (जंत्री) was in progress. The subject Jantri is very complex. Some of the Laws and Revenue Acts are very old and have become outdated or irrelevant in the prevailing situations. For the amendment and abolishment of such laws, it is obvious that the Revenue machineries have to be active with me, then only, the task can be made possible. I discussed with Mr. Prajapati, over there, about the statements and work of survey in 'Jantri'. He was very accurate in his knowledge. His explanations and clarifications about the system, process and practice on the subjects were so deep and detailed. He explained it in a very simple way, even any common citizen can understand it easily. I was much satisfied about his working and performance.

As I was just to proceed ahead from that place, Mr. Prajapati came forward and requested, "Madam, I beg your pardon. I have a request to put before you. May I tell?"

"Yes, yes, why not, you are welcome. Please open up." I said.

He hesitatingly stated, "Madam, since the last three months, my salary payment is not made by the department." I was shocked to hear that and asked for the details and the reasons for it. Friends, why such things should happen to an employee like Mr. Prajapati, who works sincerely, accurately and systematically for the Department?

I further asked him about the matter, "Madam, despite my several requests and representations, no body listens to me. Till today, I did not get my salary for the last three months. Without any reason, my transfer was done elsewhere, but here, when they realised the necessity of my expertise, I was called back but my salary payment is still in doldrums."

I knew that his superior officer had transferred him elsewhere. After Mr. Prajapati reported at the place of his transfer, there the work of Jantri was started. The work was stopped and the process became stagnant. He was then called back here, because no other person was as conversant with the work of Jantri, as

Mr. Prajpati was. He was having deep experience and expertise in the work since long. He came back and was assigned again the work of Jantri. Before that period, he worked elsewhere for three months.

Friends, every employee has his family and has a responsibility towards it. In any sort of exigency, proper care and concern are important for the employee. Now friends, you see the tragedy in this case. During the period of transfer, Mr. Prajapati did not receive his salary but he had to incur the expenses as two of his married daughters were pregnant. Household expenses also increased. He had to just try to meet the two ends. For that he had to borrow or had to manage money from other sources. This was really a disappointing situation for Mr. Prajapati.

Friends, now it was my turn for action. I immediately instructed his officer to see that the salary of Mr. Prajapati must reach to his account within 15 days. He must be paid his salary on regular basis. A person working with sincerity and commitment to his duties should get his rights on regular basis. Harassment in any case cannot be tolerated. And to my surprise, within a week, Shri Prajapati informed me, "Madam, thanks a lot and very kind of you. I received my salary for all three mounts."

In the administrative fold and within employee's cadre, there are people who work efficiently and devotedly, but due to recklessness on the part of some top level officials and because of their deficiencies and prejudice, the dedicated employees in lower cadre are disappointed. Therefore, to keep the work culture and dedication intact, such mentality must be shun and injustice to efficient employees must not be done.

2 × 1 = 2
2 × 2 = 4
2 × 3 = 6
2 × 4 = 8
2 × 5 = 10
2 × 6 =

One who Ignites a Sense of Pride in his Pupil is a Guru

Discipline in life as well as during learning, is the golden advice from our Gurus. In schools and colleges, when students are taught about discipline by the principal or teachers, some take it as a punishment. But those who obey it, their future and life get bright. To move speedily on the right track, the road and direction shown by our Guru in schools, are easy to follow.

For paving the path of discipline in the students, the institutions must frame the rules. With proper adherence to such rules, students can build up their excellent career and progressive life.

Once I was to witness a function for awarding the excellency and achievement of the students, who passed their examinations for 10th and 12th standards. For me, it is always interesting to enjoy the inspiring response from such toppers. Here also I was eagerly awaiting for their expression of thoughts and their dreams. Everyone was asked to deliver a short speech. I firmly feel that this event is of utmost importance to know. "How the role of a principal and teacher can provide for fruitful transformation in the life of a student."

A boy who stood first at the Board examination of 12th Arts, stepped up the stage to offer his expressions. He put his words proudly, "I was studying in a primary school at my village. In attendance, I was rather regular, but used to occupy the last bench and would harrass my teacher by playing mischief in classroom and on the ground of the school. I was never attentive to the lessons and would not do the homework. Instead I would just pluck the plants and flowers on the ground and indulge in eve-teasing of girls. Despite my deeds, they never failed me but promoted me to the next standard every year because my father was **Sarpanch** of the village. Out of his status or influence, I was enjoying privileged treatment at the school. Year after year, I reached up to the seventh standard. I was not willing to step up to 8th class but I was admitted to a High school in a nearby village.

It was my first day at the high school. Our class teacher entered the class from the front door. I just moved out from the back door. My exit from the class was successful, but the principal caught hold of me and took me to his office. Inquiring about my name and village, he told me in very gentle words, "Well my son, your father is a Sarpanch, a leading person in your village, is it true? Then, why should you remain behind in learning? From a far away village are you not coming to study? Why did you try to run out from the class? Did you have any urgent work to attend?" I was ashamed a lot and replied, "Sir, please pardon me, but I really dislike to study further." Patting me on my back, the principal said, "Oh, no, my son, you are a clever boy. Don't be shy of your slow learning. Don't underestimate yourself. I will help you. Do one thing from tomorrow onwards. Before going to the class, you first come to me daily! O.K.? Are you ready? and I nodded in the affirmative. From the very next day, my attendance in the school and the class became regular. My daily visit to the principal's office made me more responsible towards study, and if on any day I forgot to see him, he would enter my class and ensure that I was in the class and attentive to my lessons. My teachers also were taking care of me with their due concentration. Slowly and gradually, my mind was getting a good grip on study. With regular lesson-work and daily attendance in the classroom, I became able to pick up the perfection in all subjects. Every year I come out with good numbers and in standard 10th it was the year of climax for me. All went well and I stood first at the school. The result was really inspiring for my further study. All my teachers started to pay more attention on me. My principal was more confident on my progress. He was kind enough to keep me at his home for providing me with good lesson and tuitions. My time in travelling, up and down, from my village was thus saved. Extra time was being allotted by all my teachers, and my joy just knew no bounds. The talent and skill in me were unveiled by them. Day by day, my will to perform well was getting stronger and stronger and my hard work along with them all made an excellent way ahead for me. I fared well with flying colours. Today, I am standing before you with pride and prestige for my parents, school, my teachers and my respected principal. They all are like God to me. I bow my head before them all. Without their kindness, efforts and guidance, where would I have been? If I could not get them in time? I was just a loafer, useless and a bad boy. They transformed my life, fate and career from zero to hero." He concluded and the clappings from the audience continued for long.

Friends, the words from Raju were full of truth, transparency and innocence. It is fully true that the teachers and principals at the school are the real mentors for the students. They only can lead the students towards progress. They can pave the way to the betterment of their career. Here is an inspiring example of Raju. To get a sparkling diamond, one has to cut, sharpen and shape the stone with sufficient efforts. The one who makes his pupil feel proud is a real Guru.

Elders should not Overlook

In the society, each one is having a unique nature. Many a time, people get deceived in understanding the difference between bad and good. Such incidences mostly happen with the girls going to school or colleges. They get trapped in the temptation of money and unknowingly destroy their life. It is absolutely necessary to teach tough lessons to such wicked persons. Many innocent daughters may get saved from destroying their lives, if the elders do not overlook the information they receive and act with promptness.

Friends, I am telling this on the basis of my vast and varied experiences of 30 years of teaching at Mohinaba Kanya Vidyalaya in Amdavad. Passing through many phases, I had occasions to go deep in the life of many girls and had helped them in coming out from difficult situation. The incidences are numerous, events are endless, under which I have faced many types of problems to show them the real directions in their lives.

One day in Mohinaba School, some girls entered the teacher's room hurriedly, before the school started.

"Madam, Madam, please come quickly. Parul is weeping too much." It was still a time for starting the class. Parul was in her classroom. I promptly reached there. Parul was crying.

I asked, "Parul, what is the matter? Why are you crying." In adolescent girls, normally with growing age, many complications with their health are bound to rise. She, in reply to my asking, started weeping more. I again said, "Parul, tell me all. Unless you speak something, how will I know about your trouble?"

She then gave an envelope in my hand which she was holding while weeping.

I opened it and came to know the details. Very near to our Mohinaba School, a college was there. The envelope was handed over to Parul by one professor from that college. While putting that cover in her hand, the professor conveyed her that the same was given by her **masa,** the husband of her Aunt (Mother's Sister), who was also a professor at the college. Very casually Parul took the envelope and opened it after coming to school. To her surprise, she found a love letter in pink paper and Rupees five thousand cash kept in that envelope.

I took the covered envelope in my custody, took out the letter from it and read it. I asked Parul to calm down, and also asked her to see me after the classes were over. I then went to my class telling her not to worry and study in class attentively.

In the evening, after the school was over, myself and Parul started for her house. I knew Parul's father. He was a professor in another college. After meeting him, we discussed the matter in detail and asked Parul, "Will you be able to recognise the person who gave this envelope to you?" Parul said "Yes Madam."

Now we planned for an action on the second day. Parul's father arranged a watch on the bus-stand from where Parul used to return home by the bus. After 15 days, the fellow, who had given the envelope, appeared at the bus-stand. He boarded the bus and Parul gave the signal to the watch-keepers, waiting at the stand. They also boarded the bus to travel with the suspect. As soon as Parul alighted the bus at her stop, the suspect also got down. The watch keepers, on following the signal from Parul, caught hold of him and gave him a severe beating and handed him over to the police.

Detailed information was obtained. According to the information received the culprit was a government employee. Parul's father met his superior at his office and told everything. The superior confirmed that the fellow was a loafar, "We receive many complaints against him. You have done a good job."

Friends, such incidents are common now-a-days in the society. The elders and parents should not take them lightly or overlook them. We must be attentive, serious and quick to take timely action. Only then the safety and security of our daughters can be ensured. Such culprits in the society will also learn the lesson when our daughters become brave enough to face them courageously.

"Nobody likes an ever-crying person, and at the same time, an ever-smiling person is never a hurdle in anyone's life."

A Dead Daughter and Her Trader Father

In our society, father of a daughter is called the most humble human creature. He has to bear a lot and remain silent. We feel a lot of sympathy, in real sense, for him. In today's time, nothing will work except the tool of education given in the hands of our daughters.

We, as parents, always dream about her ideal and happy life at her **in-laws' house**. Every parent in the society has the inner intent to make their daughters feel happy in the family life.

No doubt, we sometimes come across such incidents and events, which are very shocking, sad and exciting. With the happening of such incidences, we realise how much and to what extent the people exploit others under the excuse of sympathy, kindness and co-operation. I was immensely shocked on hearing about one such incident, which could not be erased ever from the wide canvas of my mind.

The incidence was of the day when I took up my duties as a principal at Mohinaba Girls' School. One professor from a college in Amadavad comes to me and requests, "Anandiben, please favour me for a fair cause. My daughter has to appear in examination for 12th standard, but the date has lapsed to submit the form. We are already late and therefore, I request you to help us in the matter." I then asked to ascertain the situation, "I think your daughter got married and she is happy in her family with her child. Why do you want her to study further?" On my stern asking, the professor becomes emotional and starts weeping. He, with his very humble words, starts narrating the details, "As the family was good and prosperous, the boy was the only son in the family with their own accommodation in a city like Amadavad, I thought it was an ideal match for my daughter. Thinking that the daughter will be happy and will get settled under our direction and care, the marriage was arranged. Later, Daughter was gifted with a son."

I then intervened, "Very nice, your daughter is happy with her family. As she stays nearby, she can keep on visiting you often. All of you are now comfortable." He was anxious to tell further. "But, Madam, she has been driven out from her house. Nowadays she stays with us, with her little child. We, therefore, wish that her further study may fetch her a good job, after completion of her graduation. Hoping that her future life can be improved, I wish her to appear for the exam." Professor concluded the main point of his request.

Friends, it becomes much painful to me when I hear the story of troubles for any of our daughters. In this case, I extended essential help for filling up the form, and with my usual concern and habit, I reminded him, "Henceforth, let her complete the studies and start her career. Do not allow her to leave the studies in between. Do not send her to her in-laws' house forcibly and without her will."

She appeared for exam, worked hard to complete her studies in college and with the passage of time, the incident was a past tense for me.

Since the last 3-4 days, I was engaged in the activities for my party and today, the same professor appeared before me with unhappy and sad feelings on his face. I asked, "How do you do? Is anything special? Is your daughter O.K.? How you happened to come here?" And the professor looked painfully at me and said, "Anandiben, I am here for your help, again," his eyes got wetted.

"Why? What happened?" I asked anxiously. He started narrating the tragic story of his dearest daughter.

"Madam, some relatives from her in-laws' house approached us to take her back. They were talking very sweetly and in a humble way assuring us that they will put aside some property in her name. A separate house they will provide and so on. I was impressed to believe their talks innocently, thinking that, the daughter's future will take a turn. On the day before Raksha Bandhan, she departed for her in-laws' house. But again the destiny deceived us. On the very second day, that is, on Raksha Bandhan morning, her dead body was found in her bathroom. We reached there. Postmortem report revealed that she was given poison. "Bahenji, today is the fourth day of her death. Nobody has been arrested yet. I have lost my daughter. She will never be back, but I must teach them a lesson. Severe punishment to all of them is the only lesson to be taught so that others do not follow such shameful acts."

I got stunned hearing the story. How such incidents are taking place in our society? I quickly took the decision to proceed further in the matter. I approached the members of Dharti Vikas Mandal. It is a women's welfare association, actively working against domestic harassment. The ladies wing of Dharti Vikas Mandal was very powerful in protecting the rights of women, and for that, social awareness camps and campaigns were being arranged. Immediately, on the second day of intimation, a rally was organised against the government by that mandal, in co-ordination with BJP. They also organised rallies and *dharnas* daily at different places and areas. The relatives of her in-laws' side were linked with the government, but despite the fact that the opposition was so strong, arrest was done ultimately and they were presented before the court by the police. In the court campus also we, thousands of women, agitated and expressed our anger. With the result justice was done for the time being. The relatives like mother-in-law, father-in-law and husband of the daughter were put behind bars.

We believed that the accused will be punished by the court. In the course of judgement, it may take time. We worked to deliver condolence to the father of daughter for her untimely death and felt satisfied but the more shocking event was to yet happen which was beyond anybody's imagination. Time kept running, days were passing. I was sitting in the library and referring to the magazines. In one of the magazines, I noticed an article, a small one. The title was amazing—**Father sold out dead body of his daughter**. I could not stop my curiosity to read it. While reading it in detail, I found that it was about the same daughter for whom we agitated, organised rallies and represented for demanding justice. We took trouble for awakening the society. But with deep grief, it was mentioned in the article that the professor father of that daughter, made a shameful compromise in the case and accepted an offer to have a school in compensation for settlement of the suit. Apart from taking back the 'Kariyavar' of his daughter, the ugly professor took lakhs of Rupees as a deal for the dead daughter and recovered the cost even for her footwear, till she was at his house. What a shame on this greedy man who sold his own dead daughter by compromising and having material things in the bargain!

Friends, just imagine, how it would have hurted me? Think about those thousands of sisters who initiated the massive movement just to accord her the justice. Imagine about the soul of that daughter, who died due to harassment, and about the shameless act by the professor from whom we expect the lessons for value-based education. Instead of fulfilling the hopes and our expectations, he blemished his own reputation. Do the so-called gentleman in the society worry in matters like this? I am just unable to express my feelings.

"In what we are
more interested?
In opening up,
In keeping us open to others
or in exposing others?"

Duties of Parents Towards their School-going Children

A child spends 5 or 6 hours during a day in the school. So many other things, the child perceives from the atmosphere and ambience around him/her. It is therefore expected of the parents that they keep themselves aware about the activities of their children all the time and when they are outside the school. In today's times of television serials, some programmes on TV seem to attack on Indian civilization and culture and the bad impact of this adversely sets in the tender minds of our children. We think that the atmosphere and culture at our home and in the family are good, but the bad company outside the home takes the little ones towards bad habits. Generally, our children, while leaving the home for school or college, take our permission or inform us about their programmes for going out. We presume that our child is going for studies, but it is not so always in all the cases. Parents must set their eyes on every activity of their child. It is time to remain alert.

I mention here one incident as an eye-opener for parents. It was the morning time for the school. The children had already reached their classes. One little daughter came to me with her mother. She came to take her school bag from my office. Out of her fear to enter the office of the Principal, she came in along with her mother. For me, it was a matter of relief as I was to ask her for bringing her mother to me. Now, her mother had came here of her own. She told, "Madam, yesterday my daughter forgot her bag after attending to the cleanliness work in the class. She will now go to her class after taking her bag from here. Madam, she was afraid of you for her silly mistake and brought me here with her." I told her mother, looking towards them both." It is good that you came along with her, even otherwise I thought of calling you."

Friends, before they came to my office, one gentleman had come and given that bag to me. While putting the bag before me, he gave me the information which was very crucial, "Yesterday afternoon, a girl from the school was sitting on the bench of the garden, with one boy. She left her bag there only, as if she had forgotten to take it along, after meeting with the boy and both walked away."

The school bag which was lying there in the garden was noticed by that gentleman. He took the bag and verified the books inside it. As the name of the school was there on the books, he came here and handed it over to me. I at that time noted the name and address of that gentleman and also got a statement from him about how he had got the bag from the garden, in writing.

I started questioning her mother, "At what time she returns home? Yesterday at what time she came? If she was late, why did you not ask her or inquired in the school?"

Her mother remained silent. She did not have any answer. Now it was the turn of the girl to face the questions. "Beta, tell me the truth and truth only. Did you really forget your school bag in the class? The cleaning work in the classroom is being done by the other friends of yours. Nobody from them came to handover your bag at the office. Now tell me where did you forget the bag?" Now, how did she dare to speak, as I was steadily looking at her, and her eyes were set down on the ground. I then asked, "You had forgotten your bag not in the classroom but in the garden, is it so?"

Her mother now suddenly was taken aback on hearing this and argued, "Madam, what are you saying? She is my daughter! How can she be in the garden?

I said to her in a strict tone, "Yes, it was your daughter sitting yesterday noon in the garden. Here is the proof," and showed her the note from that gentleman and the bag. "See it properly, is this her bag or not?" She read that note and started abusing her daughter, "You liar! Where were you yesterday? With whom were you in the garden? Why you did not return directly to home?"

I then asked her to calm down and said, "We must keep a track of the arrival and out time of our daughters. See that at what time she leaves for school and be sure about her time of return. We must know that in the age of adolescence, the girls are experiencing various feelings. We must take specific care of their behaviour. Parents, and particularly mothers, should be a bridge between the school and the home. Then only we will be able to save them and show them the right path of life."

The Joy of Witnessing A Widow-Marriage

Fortunately, now our society is gradually getting free from various social evils, after facing them for a long time, but new problems are also coming up spoiling our society. There was once a time when widow marriage was looked upon with disrespect. Where a tradition for child marriage prescribed, the ratio of child widows was high. But now our daughters are leading in learning. They have the stronger tool of education in their hands. There is no insecurity or helplessness in them. Even today people are not ready and willing to accept re-marriage of widows. I still remember an incident occured some 30-40 years ago.

It is too difficult to come out from the clutches of bad customs and wrong beliefs. When things get rooted in the society, to fight against such evils is a very difficult process. Constant combating, courage and strong resolve towards principles only can lead to good results. Other aspects like sanctity and clarity in conduct and character play important roles for fetching a fair and fruitful outcome. My heart still becomes joyous when I recall and recollect the memories in which I was instrumental to initiate a widow marriage in the society. At that time, the community was happy to feel proud of me.

The incident is an interesting one. A little girl Shanta became a *Balika Vadhu*. She got married in her childhood. She was still to know the meaning of marriage. Shanta did not know the meaning of relations like *Naṇad* and *Saas*! She was yet to understand a person called Husband! Before she could understand such relations, she was at house of her in-laws. Somehow, Shanta completed a year at her husband's house. Unluckily her husband became victim of scorpian bite and Shanta became a child-widow. All her hopes and dreams shattered. Education to her was the only ray of hope. Central government at that time was running a 'Condensed Course' for widows for their studies. I was looking after a **Nari Vikas Griha** at Visnagar city and for that reason, the responsibility to run the condensed course was with me.

We had many such sisters like Shanta; some were little elder and studied up to 5th standard. Even older women were admitted to the course. The duration of the course was two years. Study was rather tough with the reason that many of them had left the learning years long before. They had forgotten everything. Our efforts were to bring them back slowly on the track of learning. On one hand, they had to tackle their poverty, while on the other hand, they were helpless widows.

All were much worried about their future life, and the tragic thoughts about their setting in the family, in absence of the husbands. All of them were used to pass their day-time, in study, but at night, all sisters were passing time in exchanging the stories of their self-living. Sometimes, they used to weep while narrating the tragic talks about their troublesome life. At the other moment, they became hopeful of their new life. Days passed and time elapsed. Their examination arrived. Many of them successfully went through. Of those, some got their jobs at primary school and started earning, and came up with their head high, and stayed tight in self-reliant way with the society. Shanta was one of them. She attained the age of 22 years. I felt always disturbed to see Shanta in her widow attire.

Once Shanta came to meet my elder sister. She talked to my sister. It was about her wish to remarry a person. The fellow was a young widower, staying at the village where Shanta was posted. He was eager to marry her. His family as well as the villagers were also agreeable to their marriage. My elder sister was convinced. For Shanta, it was an opportunity to get rid of the life of helpless widow. She thought, 'When a well-set person wants me as his wife, the proposal was not bad.' Shanta got ready. The relatives of the young man gave their consent. I was also already aggrieved by the evil of opposing blindly widow marriage; I found the case of Shanta to be in proper perception. We got their marriage arranged tactfully and registration for it was done in due course. Both entered the village with their holy bonding of a happy marriage.

During the vacation, Shanta did not visit her parents place. We were also at our village. Shanta's brother came to our house after two-three days. He said—"During this vacation, my sister did not come to our home and I had come to know that she got married in that village. She has spoiled our image. How a widow in our society can marry again? Sister, you come with us, we will go there with fifty men and bring her back to our house. She has just left us disparate and shameful in our community."

Friends, as we all were knowing the fact because Shanta's marriage was arranged under our witness and wish, we talked very nicely with Shanta's brother and tried to gain time. We explained to him, "See, your suggestion is right but at present, they are not in the village. We all will go there together after two days." We then got the time for the settlement of the problem.

I then went to Visnagar and intimated Shanta about the anger of her brother. I wrote to her, "He may come there with his men. He is against your marriage. So, please be careful. Now there is vacation. You both stay away from your house." We thought time is always remedial. Some time gap makes the matter peaceful and calm. It will be possible to settle the problem thereafter.

Shanta's brother came to the village after two days, along with his fifty men. According to the talk we had, they all arrived by a bus. People here in the village were also well-prepared. Both the sides, after beating the bush, and exchanging harsh words, were about to indulge in mutual fighting and scuffle, but in meanwhile the police arrived. There was an excitement and demand to make Shanta to be present before them. Lots of chaos and exchange of hot words were taking place, but we were not to give up. We found that our strategy was leading to success, and we were all prepared to make it at any cost.

Friends, the main character Shanta was not present on the spot. How could she appear there? Our expectation was clear. Both of them loved each other, and decided to get married for keeping their company lifelong. Then what was wrong and unfair in it?

As the quarrel was going on, some wise and prudent people of village had a visit to the place. On hearing the facts, they also gave their opinion in favour of Shanta, the marriage of this couple has taken place after they obtained the consent of the entire village and they have now settled in the society." They just proposed it now in such words as if they openly favoured the married couple. On their scolding to Shanta's brother and his companions, we also joined the wise persons of the village, and indirectly tried to calm him down. Everyone in the village knew that we were supporters of Shanta.

The matter settled down gradually. In those days, it was first widow-marriage in the society and in the area. It was a very strong traditional belief that the girl if happens to become widow in very young age, she then has no choice but to pass her life lonely and without a companion in life. She had to remain in the dark corner of her house. No question of remarriage was to arise otherwise the image of the family would be ruined in the community.

Friends, see the tragic side of the logic. If the man becomes widower after his wife is dead, he can remarry and have a new wife. Society was never taking any objection to it. But when a young daughter under tradition of child-marriage unfortunately becomes widow, she loses every right of her life and livelihood. Her remaining life was left to doldrums—without any companion, without any dream for future, and like all darkness even in the day. How cruel was that society? How strange and severe were the social rules? Why such double standards existed for a female in the society?

Fortunately, now the ladies are coming up gradually, and coming forward fearlessly. They have become brave to fight against the unfair customs and old traditions. Nowadays widow marriages are being celebrated joyfully and enthusiastically in auspicious and encouraging way in almost all communities.

"No matter the height of the mountain of Elevation remains uncertain, but the depth of the bottom of collapse must be ascertained."

Determination, Courage and Clear Vision helped

In today's advanced and modern age, many a time rituals and traditional bindings in the community become barriers to development and progress. When you give good education to your daughter, it is difficult to find a proper and educated young man in the smaller society or in a compact community. The anxiety is ever mounting up for the parents of such daughters. They have to keep thinking always till the ultimate selection is made. Today the problem is less severe due to the feeling of *'Vasudhaiva Kutumbkam'*, yet the cast-related restrictions still persists at various places. The parents may make the future of their children secure if they act with courage and firm resolve at a proper time.

Here is an incident which took place thirty years back at Sipor village in Mehsana district. Ramila was a clever student. Due to encouragement from her father, she studied well and became an engineer.

At that time, as per the code of conduct prevalent in the community, every family must arrange the matrimonial relations for the children within the fold of their own community. Ramila's father was well-educated. Every father does have emotional attachment with his daughter. He was worried for the marriage of his Engineer daughter Ramila. We in their village were having good relations with the family. As and when he happened to visit our house, he used to express his grief for not getting well-educated groom in the community for her educated daughter. He did not have the courage to arrange her marriage outside his own community. We, in our talks and discussion on such an issue, used to provide him the guts and courage to come out against the community. "What more the society will do? At the most, they can put you out of their fold. Ramila is well-educated and has a good career. For her marriage, a young, well-cultured and educated boy should be selected."

Meanwhile, one day Ramila's father came to our house with a good news, "The boy is a doctor, bio-data is good. The parents and the family of the boy do not have any objection to caste and religion. They also prefer a girl having good job and education. Ramila qualifies for both, she is also ready."

And despite strong opposition of their community, we all were very firm to finalise the function of ring ceremony. It was arranged with ease.

After some time the date was fixed for Ramila's marriage, but during those four months, Ramila's father and his family had to face the opposition and objections from the society and relatives. They were threatened that their family will be boycotted from the community and from the village if the marriage was not cancelled. But all were firm and took up the challenge of becoming the front-runners of the society.

It was now time for the wind to blow for social reform. The situation was critical but the courage, clear vision and willpower were with us. Our side was becoming stronger with resolve to resist the odds. We decided to arrange the ceremony of wedding at Amadavad. Invitations were distributed in the villages. Other miscellaneous works were done by friends like us. The marriage took place with great pomp and show. Catering was a complete feast, nobody was to complain at least. Ramila was given a warm bidding to the house of in-laws. On successful completion of the event, we all took the breath of ease.

It was too difficult to stand against the social system and tradition 30 years ago. But this was essential for social reform and for establishing new ideology towards new era of progress. We can observe it everywhere that there are many such daughters from society who have given up narrow views which prevailed earlier. The couple is now dwelling in happiness and joy with proper partners in life.

"A good rain gives a meaning to the hard-work of the farmer, in the same way, good atmosphere makes efforts of a seeker a success."

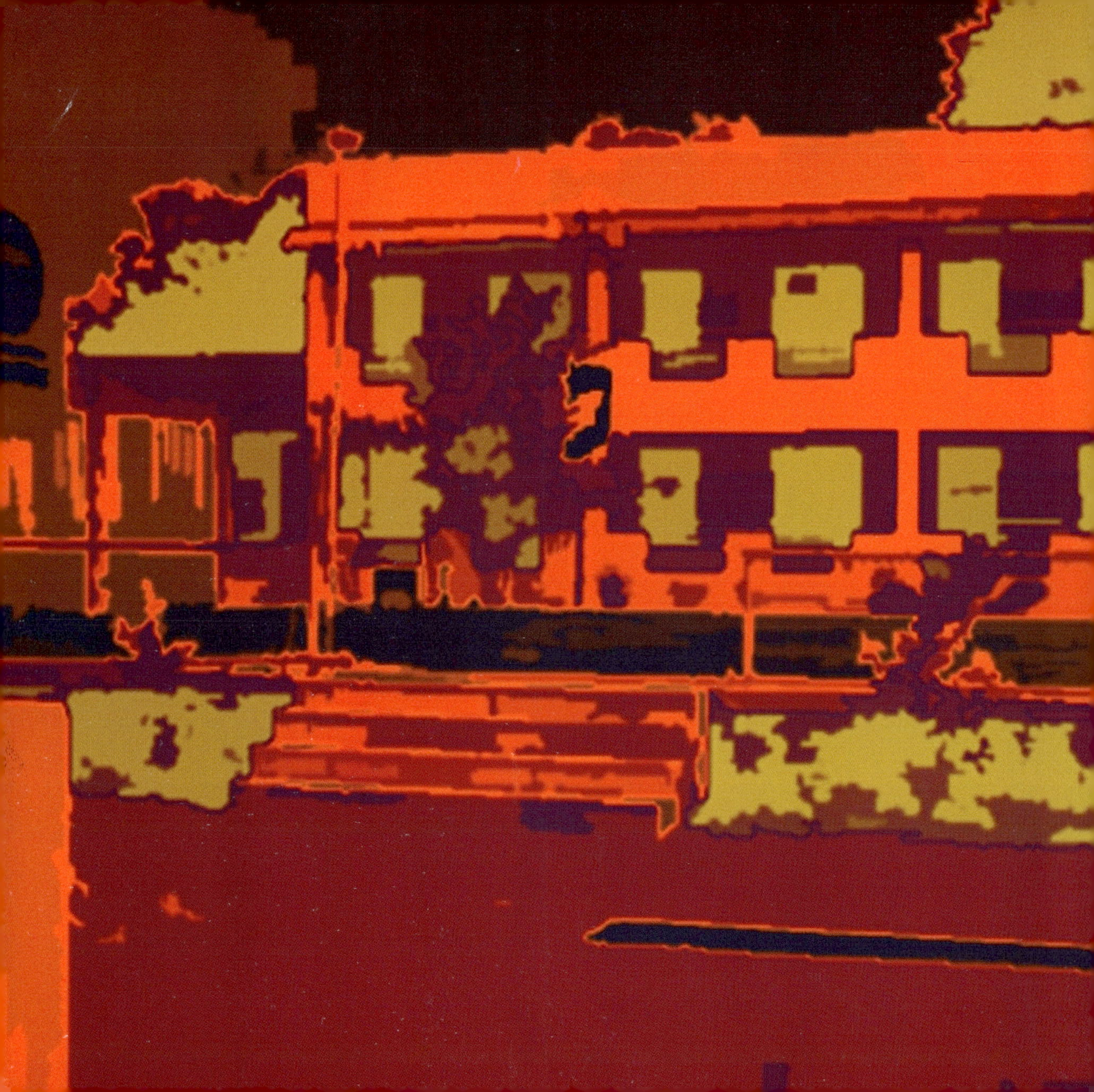

I Proved Myself as a Principal

There is no option to hard work. Every step towards success demands lots of drops of our sweat. We have to toil constantly to get our goal. Circumstances may be too tough but the life is fighting the odds, facing the challenges fearlessly and keep moving forward to achieve targets.

After completing my B.Ed. and M.Sc. during the year 1967-68, I joined Mohinaba Kanya Vidyalaya as a teacher. In the same year, Minaxi Desai joined as a P.T. teacher. We happened to meet while sitting in the Teachers' room. Our friendship became more intense and took the shape of inner intimacy. She no longer remained a friend only but I treated her as my younger sister. Being a Science teacher, my salary was higher. She was drawing less as a P.T. teacher. One day I said to her, "First you complete your B.A. and pass the degree for B.Ed., then get you will have higher salary."

She was Anavil-Brahmin by caste. Her family was poor. The responsibility of her younger brother and sister was on her shoulder. After P.T.C., she could not continue with her studies. Much time had lapsed since she left the studies. Due to growing age, her marriage could not take place; and that was her prime worry. She was staying along with her brother and sister. I insisted her to fill the form for F.Y. B.A. She started going to college after teaching at school. She used to study hard and worked all the day relentlessly. In the school, during free period, I used to teach and provide her with necessary guidance. Other teachers were also helpful to her. She appeared for exam and got a good result. Everyone praised her for her performance. Because of her good image as a student, and prime role in other activities, she became popular in her community also.

She then married one Ulhas Desai working in a textile mill. She was burdened with the responsibilities of her mother-in-law, father-in-law and the entire family. In the school also, she remained sincere to share the responsibilities. With such enormous burden, she broke down. She became victim of hypertension and depression. I gave her the courage, "Minaxiben, don't get upset or sad. Everything will be ok soon. I myself also had studied in such situations. Don't leave your studies in between, keep it up and continue your studies."

I went to her house and convinced her mother-in-law. She agreed to help her in daily household work. When the examination for B.A. was on the way, her father-in-law expired. She kept the courage and appeared for exam. She got through successfully and stepped up one more platform with much struggle. During the period, she delivered a baby son.

Then she completed B.Ed. Now her salary increased substantially. After two years, the number of students in the school decreased and she was declared as an extra teacher. She had to go to another school. While leaving our school to join another school, she was very sad and was in tears on the day of her farewell.

"Anandiben, today I feel that I am being separated from my friends. I will miss you all. How will it be possible to meet you daily?" In the meantime, 6 to 7 years passed by but our friendship was intact. She decided to prepare for M.A. and completed it. I became Principal of my school. Several old teachers retired. We had some vacancies in the faculty. So, I made a proposal to the trustee-management for calling back Minaxiben at our school. But they were not willing to take her back. When a Principal has to take decision in the interest of the school and students, the ego of management or trustees, generally comes in the way. The school is ours; we have a right to do as we want. Such mentality cannot be changed easily. The vision and determination of a Principal plays a crucial role in the interest of the school.

In the school, it was necessary to recruit and appoint some teachers. Bhavanaben was the candidate. She was related to one of the trustees, and he was trying to accommodate her as a teacher of English subject. It was now my turn to react as a Principal. I put a condition before the trustee's board. "See, as per the rule, Minaxiben should be recalled first. Secondly, Bhavanaben does not possess the required qualification to work as a teacher of English." I put down my views strongly. Now the trustees were puzzled: what is to be done? Interaction, consent and consultation could not resolve the tangle. I was never in favour of undue dealings and settings. Therefore, my stand was firm.

Ultimately, the trustees agreed to take Minaxiben back in the school. But they put a condition before me. "First the order should be issued for Bhavanaben." I smelt something fishy about their intention. I could not trust them. The tussle continued. I assured them that Bhavanaben will also get the order. At last, they agreed. First Minaxiben, and later Bhavanaben was issued letters to join the school.

Minaxiben was overjoyed with tears as she was coming to her original place. Some people greeted my administrative success as a shrewd step, but in the test of maintaining friendship and in the insistence for ideology, I fared well. It was my real joy and a matter of inner satisfaction.

Later on, Minaxiben became Principal of Mohinaba School and I became the Education Minister of the State. Even today, our friendship is same as it was before. It is easy to make friends but difficult to maintain. Friendship never gets affected by factors like designation, status, place, time and situations. Of course, sometime we feel that to have real friends is the feast of our fate. But forming our fate is a matter in our hands.

Taught A Tough Lesson To That Loafer

Many a times if the children understand the position of their parents, problems may stop raising their head. I will cite an incident here when I took charge as principal at Mohinaba Kanya Vidyalaya.

It was time for recess. The girls parked their cycles at the campus and when they came for their breakfast, there were some chits found on some of the cycles. The chits were not merely pieces of papers but carried a three-word sentence. "I love you" was written on every such piece of paper. The girls got afraid to see such mischief played at the campus and came immediately running to my office. I asked them to remain calm.

"Go to your class rooms, and have your breakfast. Don't get worried at all. I will find out who is the culprit!"

Generally, on happening of incidence like this we register police complaints, but I for this did not do it. Such problems are sensitive and serious. Sometimes without referring them to police system, importance is accorded only for their solutions. I, therefore, decided to take up the issue in my hand, without referring it to police for its solution.

First of all, I dialed the phone number, written in those pieces of papers. I began to talk over phone, pretending in tone and voice of a girl, just talking on the phone. I was sure that the culprit may be sitting on phone presuming that someone will definitely respond to his note which he put up on cycles. Something happened like that and my phone was picked up by that boy only.

I said, "I got your chit, but dear, where shall we meet?" He immediately responded, "Oh dear, please reach G.E.B. office, Naranpura at 2 o'clock. I will be there." But, how am I to recognise you? Some other boys may also be there?" Talking in such a fashion I found out about the colour of the shirt he would be wearing. The fellow was a compounder at a private clinic. I made it sure that he was the boy whom we were searching for.

At about 12 o'clock, I again phoned him, by changing the voice, "When can I meet the Doctor? I am his patient and want his contact number." When I got the number for the Doctor, I connected him. "Doctor! do you know what your compounder is doing outside? Please come at so and so place at 2 o'clock. Do not do anything; just wait and watch what your compounder is doing there."

Exactly at 2 o'clock, on my luna motorbike, I reached the place opposite G.E.B. office. The 'road Romeo' was standing there waiting for that girl. I caught hold of him. The Doctor also reached there in time. He slept him thrice, and scolded him saying, "Rascal, spoiling the image of my clinic? You are fired henceforth." The road Romeo was now on road without job and was rusticated from the college where he was studying.

After two months of this incident, one poor old man came to my house. I asked him to sit. Offered him tea and water to drink. Asked him why he came. In reply, all of a sudden the poor man started weeping loudly. I could know that he was the father of that Romeo. He had come here to apologise for the behaviour of his son, and started requesting, "Madam, the boy whom you caught hold of is my son. Please forgive him for his faults. I assure you sister that henceforth he will not do such acts. I have thrashed him and scolded him heavily. I am a poor farmer, do my farming and pay his fees for study. He was earning little from the job of a compounder but due to his bad company, he went the wrong way down. It is good that he has been punished but now he is feeling sorry for it. Please sister, forgive him, and be kind enough to save his life from being ruined."

I felt too much for his father. I then remembered the quote which was taught in the school, "Do confess your deeds, the stream of forgiveness has arrived from Heaven. Any sinful act of yours may be washed away by the prayer from you inner soul." I, therefore, forgave that Romeo on the request of his father. Friends, the tale of tragedy and confession made my conscious kind to forgive him.

The parents who are toiling a lot for their children, but sometimes it is not understood in proper sense by the children. Their way towards the right direction in life gets diverted. In the society, there may be many young boys who are on the verge of spoiling their lives.

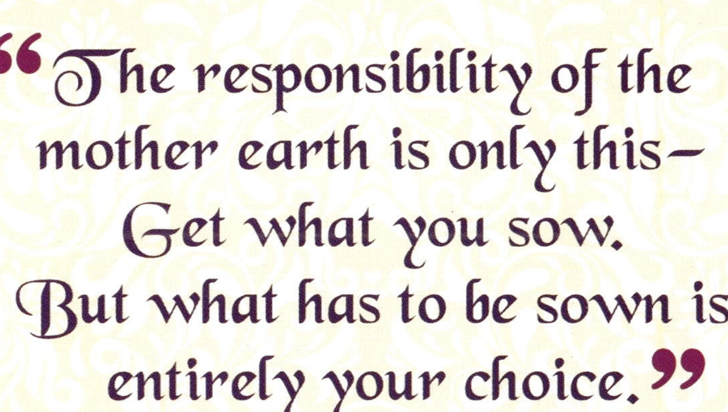

Do Listen to the Grief of Committed Workers

We feel pity on such people who opine randomly or talk low about the persons active in politics or in public life. Such opinions are based on their senseless thinking and ignorance of the facts. Such things create agony and anger in the minds of people who work benevolently in the service of common man or the masses. During my political career, I had come across so many gems of humanity who remained neatly committed to social service in their public life. They remained ever active to serve without caring for their personal joy, happiness or comforts. It hurts them when the society, without recognising or understanding them, keeps on criticising and commenting on them. I don't believe that there is a dearth of people committed to social service in the society, but if it is so, the situation is a matter of our concern.

I entered politics actively during the years 1986-1987. A very few women were active in politics, say hardly eight or ten, at that time in Gujarat. I took up the charge as chairperson for women front (महिला मोरचा) in Gujarat. Out of such eight or ten women, one lady, Annapurnaben was from Kalol town of district Mehsana. She was poor but hard-working. Not a single programme arranged by BJP could be completed without her help and attendance. During the elections, she would never sleep. Working through day and night, she never got tired and would fulfill her duty for her household also. She was earning her livelyhood by selling milk pouches. She was a widow. She brought up her two sons and got them married, had her grandchildren and a happy family.

On the other side, I was going to take politics as a career in a serious manner. My regular contact with Annapurnaben was cut, but her sociability, service and loyalty towards the party were the sweet memories for me. As I was a withness to it, her specific image was permanently stuck in my mind.

After a long time, I was in Kalol for a function arranged by BJP. Annapurnaben took a chance to take me to her house. I saw the condition of her house and family. One of her sons had expired, leaving his children and wife as additional responsibility on Annapurnaben. The second son was in employment on a meager pay. In the time of such a high inflation, it was too hard to run the household. After giving the help for books, fees, etc. for the children, I left but one thing disturbed me mentally thereafter—"How many such poor families may be there who are working sincerely for the party? Even under such poor conditions, they, at their own cost and expenses, remain commited to the party work. I really wondered if such families exist even today?

Time was passing. I became Education Minister. One day Annapurnaben came to my house. Looking at the expression on her face, I found that she might be facing financial crisis. She told me with tears in her eyes, "Bahen now it is too difficult to bear. It has become hard to run the house. We don't need any thing extra but expenses for the provisions for two times, to eat, are to be made. The elders may cut their food intake to one time, but how the children are to be fed two squre meals a day?" She was not able to talk further. I asked, "What happened." She continued further, "I had never asked anybody for help. But today I am here to beg for my younger son. He has obtained loan from the bank. His salary gets exhausted in repayment of the instalments. The income from sale of milk is not sufficient."

On one side, she was continuously narrating about her struggle, and on the other end, my memories of past were running on fast track. I was thinking that her contribution to party in the past made the foundations of the party firm. Her personality, full of virtues, at that time, put the party on high image. I then asked her,

"Tell me, what help you want? She said, "Nothing else, but provide us with foodgrain and other grocery items which can last at least for two years. I will pay for it after the debt of the bank is only paid. I don't want to spread my hands before anybody."

I was thinking, "A woman from a respected family. Honest and hard working, being a dedicated worker in BJP had come for help. Just imagine, what sort of mental struggle and sacrifice of self-respect she had to face, while coming here before me for help?" I immediately called my personal assistant Shri Ashokbhai to get her from market the food items, provisions and materials she asked for. Wheat, rice, oil and other provisions were ordered to reach her home. Annapurna stood up and bowed down. All help was sent to her at Kalol in my Car.

In the second year, the same help was forwarded to her at her home. In the third year, she came and said, "Bahen, thank you. Now I don't require the help any more. With which word should I thank you? Now all my debts are re-paid." She became very emotional while saying so. I just stood up and put my hands over her shoulder consoling her. "Bahen, in fact, you have inspired the people like us. Without thinking of your family, you remained dedicated for pulling up the party's image. With the core struggle by devoted workers like you, the party had progressed. You never put your poverty into picture, but remained dedicated. People like you are all our inspirations. Please rest assured, my doors are always open for you, never hesitate to knock at the doors, if you need it ever in future.

Annapurnaben left with hopes but I stood there in a sad mood, for which I had sufficient reasons. "How many such Annapurnabahens are there in our society who had done good for us, yet the society is reluctant towards them. Nobody worries for them. Society means exactly what it is – I, you and we all."

Witnessing Directly the Capability of her Offspring, which Mother will not Get Delighted

Our women have to pass through numerous odds when they accept to carry on their responsibility towards the family and children while attending to their jobs. Physical as well as mental fitness is a must for them. The double duty situation on the job and in family takes the test in setting the schedule on daily basis. At times when children are clever and wise, half of the tension gets diffused automatically. A mother may worry about her son but gets delighted when the son is competent.

This is an incident during the days when I was on job at Mohinaba School in Ahmedabad. We were staying in new pole locality of Shahpur area. Every parent has to think over twice about the admission of his/her child in the school. About the admission for my son Sanjay, I thought to put him in Gujarati medium school, but my husband insisted for his admission in a English medium school. Finally, we selected Rachana School, Shahibag for his study in English medium. The school was near our residence.

After completing his first and second standards, when Sanjay was in third standard, there were communal riots in Gujarat, particularly in Ahmedabad. With the start of riots, the schools in Ahmedabad were kept closed. Curfew was declared. My school and Rachana School were run by Kasturbhai Lalbhai group. As the situation in these areas was normal, the schools were functioning.

Myself and Sanjay were in a Autorikshaw together for the school. I dropped Sanjay at the gate of Rachana School. It was about 10 o'clock in the morning. I walked up to Laldarwaja, to catch the bus. I saw that children from Rachana School were returning. Instead of entering the school, they were coming out. I, therefore asked them, "Whether Rachana School is working or closed?" Someone answered, "Today they have declared it closed and children are given holiday." Immediately I worried for Sanjay, my son. "What will he do alone? Where will he go?" In the situation like this, obviously the heart of any mother may get entrenched into so many types of doubts, and get surrounded by unlimited uncertainties. "If anything will happen to him?" I returned to school and inquired about Sanjay. But I was shocked, my son was not there. It intensified my worries. I went inside the school for further inquiry with the peons in the school. All of them spoke at a time, "Madam, Sanjay left very early from here."

"Where my son, Sanjay will be?" I hurriedly went here and there, on the bus-stand, and to the corner of the road. Where to ask and with whom to inquire? Who can tell me about my son? "For any family, nothing is dearer to them than a child. During those days, there were no mobile phones like we have today, or no facilities for STD. There was no means of communication through which inquiry can be made at home about his whereabouts, and about his reaching home.

The situation was very worrisome for me. The worry about Sanjay was mounting up every moment, and the urgency to reach the school on regular time was in mind. I took an auto, and reached the school. Prayer was in process. As soon as the prayer was over, our principal called me. I presumed that he might have called me to ask the reason of my late-coming. I was mentally prepared for his scolding and to learn the lesson on discipline. I would suggest that for the sermon in discipline, we must have principal like Shri Daulatbhai.

As soon as I entered his office, our principal Daulatbhai said, "Bahen, your son is very clever. When he knew that school was closed, he quickly took a rikshaw and stopped it at the gate of Mohinaba School. At that time, teacher Minaxiben Desai was passing through, Sanjay shouted from rikshaw for Minaxiben and went to her. He asked her to pay the Rikshaw fare saying her, "My mummy will pay it to you later." Daulatbhai concluded.

Now I realised that the way Daulatbhai told the whole story, the tone of his talk was full of joy and pride and, friends what to tell about Minaxiben! She not only paid the Rikshaw fare, but took Sanjay inside the School. She asked Sanjay, "Beta from where did you come?" Sanjay narrated the entire story to Minaxiben. "While going to her school, mummy left me at the gate of my School. I saw the School was closed. I thought, "Mummy must have gone directly to her School" and therefore I took Rikshaw and came here."

After reaching the school, Minaxiben informed Shri Daulatbhai Desai about my late arrival at the school, because I had to wait and search for Sanjay. After knowing all the facts, Daulatbhai told me, "Bahenji your Sanjay is very clever; he came here by taking autorickshaw. We thought you might have gone home in search of your son. Therefore, I deployed our peon Lalji, to take Sanjay at your home by a rikshaw. We arranged all this before you arrived here. Now Sanjay has reached home safely. You need not worry at all, go to your class and teach your lesson without any tension."

Friends, on that day, I found that our sir, who appears so stern, was transformed into a flower in the garden-so soft & so sweet!

Sanjay was studying in standard 3rd at that time. He was hardly 7 or 8 years old. At that age, it is appreciable of him thinking about my possible movement about my reaching the School and asking Minaxiben for payment of riksha fare, etc. And the courage, quick action at a crucial time shows the maturity of his mind. Not only that, he by his action had given her mother an assurance of a specific type while witnessing direcly the capability of her son. So, which mother will not get delighted on seeing this?

A Task Full of Challenges and The Enthusiasm to Learn New Things

It is not that any higher post or bigger responsibility makes a person more competent automatically. In the job at administrative level everyday many new things are necessary to be tackled. Revenue department is such a section where we find enormous complexity of laws, acts and rules. If you want to be effective, efficient and result oriented, you must have aspirations, tacts and untried efforts at your disposal.

Friends, when I was entrusted the responsibilities for the revenue department, the problem for me was my background which till then remained of a teacher, a simple soul mainly associated with job of teaching. My activities connected with women welfare were also mainly related to education, directly or indirectly. In my entire career, education remained the base and particularly the education and progress for the women was its goal. In revenue department, the working is of specific type which needs enough expertise. Of course, I always preferred challenges. The performance which gives the opportunity for innovation has always remained enjoyable for me.

As a Minister, the officials and employees working under me were my sources of learning. Even there was an openness on my part, the caders in officer's level rather remained under the limits of protocol and respect. To learn new work is essential for our duties, and for that, the way to learn must be found out. I did the beginning. My first preference was to understand about the problems of people, the complications of laws and system in revenue rules under which they are trapped. Instead of learning about the laws, I started to study the files. Meetings and interactions with my officials helped me to understand the complaints from farmers and the landlords. I used my commonsense, utilised it while tackling the task and implementing the system in a simple way.

It was my first meeting with District Collector. Outgoing as well as incumbent, both Collectors were present. One officer from my department was also there. I had done enough homework and preparation at Gandhinagar before attending the meeting. I did very minute and meticulous preparations about the problems. Even for the supplementary questions, which may probably be asked at the meeting, I had gone in detail to fully understand the root cause of the problems, and, therefore, I was ready to deal with every matter at the meeting.

The meeting started. I began to take up each subject on agenda, one by one. In the matter of any disputed hearing, I was questioning and getting the things clarified wherever necessary. Just as 'when was the last hearing? on the basis of that hearing, what are the possibilities towards the solution? And its detail, when the next hearing was fixed? How many dates did you give?' etc.

During the discussion on the subject, it came to my notice that, seven or eight dates (Mudats) generally are to be given. I immediately asked "why to give so many dates? And for whom? The Lawyer takes away Rs. 1 to 2 thousands from the farmer! That is a loss to the poor farmers. If you can finish within three dates, why can't you complete the case on last Mudat? I also asked such question. "We ultimately work for whose benefits? For the lawyers or for the farmers who actually require the justice?"

My contention was, during the meeting with collectors, Prant officer should also remain present. Deputy Collector as well as Mamlatdar also should attend the meeting. The process then will take the rhythm. It will become easy to speedily dispose of the case by our joint efforts and by sharing the experience from each one at one place and time.

And the idea worked well. We have reached solution of many problems beyond what we expected.

Friends, it is not a new story that the pendency of the old problems in Revenue Department is very high. The past record is very discouraging in the matter of their serious and speedy disposal. I also took up that issue on the warfoot. Starting with questioning officers about the present status of the cases by actually handling them. Where the pendency is above one year, "How many files you are having for such cases." How many cases are pending beyond 6 months? What efforts did you make? I was asking each officer the status of cases, but when the officer gave a reply, that the particular file was forwarded to collector office, then my next question was to the concerned collector about the receipt of file, the time and status of it.

On receipt of the status of file, my next question to them was about the schedule of its disposal. If there is stagnancy, for what reason? Whether it was any administrative hurdle or just a policy related limitation? Or is it just a causal delay? etc.

On every matter, I used to put at least eight to ten questions, asking about the smallest details and kept on inspiring them in their performance. I also made encouraging suggestions to them. With my encouragement for their innovative suggestions, there was more enthusiasm in the employees and staff.

Questions I put before collector office, "that there may be twenty-five problems before you. Out of them, have you sent even one to the Department? If they are sent, prepare a list and give it to me, to follow up with the department." The list is being prepared. List of pending work is with you, so find out immediately about its status. This can be ascertained from time to time for taking faster and better work from any employee. All the higher authorities should have this system. This I have learnt on the basis of my experience.

There are numerous problems in the matter of issuing permission certificates to non-agricultural land. The cultivable land remained unused since a long time, no crop or produce are being taken from it. Then it becomes essential to register it for making it N.A. If the application for that purpose is received from the landlord, the period for its disposal is necessary to be fixed and made known. I, therefore, took the subject in hand. I prepared a query list, FAQs – frequently asked questions, on my own, in my mind as follows:

How many applications are received for N.A.?

How many of them were rejected? And reasons for their rejection? To submit the reasons, the officer goes to his place and brings the files. One by one, he opens the files and gives reasons for rejecting N.A. permissions. In some cases, the titles are not clear and in other, the land records show somebody else's name. The problems are noticed with such other reasons. Officers are telling the reasons in their own way, and my knowledge keeps on progressing. When I understand them clearly, I add my commonsense to it. The work may get simplified when there is eagerness and integrity with commitment.

Many a times, I do cross-checking of the matter. I go on questioning till I fully understand it, and the answer is received many times from those questions only. I tell sometimes "See, these three points are proper, but the fourth one is not to be taken in the base, why you brought it in addition?" And on going further, it comes on my query. "Tell me how much and what proof and documents you are asking for? Did you ever read the G.R. for your work? How many types of proof-documents, and subordinations are required in it? It is very clearly mentioned in it, and therefore nothing to its addition is required to be obtained."

I go on learning more and more by making many types of such questions and the answers I got from them. My learning was getting updated in the field with the result of answers for so many major and minor questions. The matters were well understood by the responsible officers that the work must be attended as per the guidelines, no deviation will be allowed. If the work is disposed of in its scheduled time, then only it has a meaning.

I have also marked often that "even if the rule permits, the officers do not take decisions for some or the other reason. The files never get cleared. If any additional question they make me, of their own, I used to write it down. If, through an oversight, any matter remained out of my knowledge, it comes in the open by this method. My enthusiasm and the eagerness for learning the work geared up nourishing the system of specific awareness and accuracy in the administrative department in my office.

I found and realised very good result from the meetings held at district levels in the State. Pendency is getting reduced. The red-tapism gets done away with. It was decided to amend the G.R. if anything is lacking or has to be added it. The process for timely enhancement of G.R. is implemented.

Friends, I started a mission for disposal of old records. The result was encouraging.

The feedback, the opinion and the responses received from the people and the government circles were. "Madam is very strict. She is accurate and her knowledge of law is excellent. She even catch-holds the loopholes of others, etc." But I was sure about my duties, which I determined to perform by learning my work devotedly. I will remove the difficulties of people in real sense. I have got the opportunity to serve the people and for that, why I should not do my best, and make sincere use of my knowledge to solve the problems of the poor and small farmers of my state?

The Biography of A Sensitive Teacher

Anandiben Patel is a peculiar personality of the public life in Gujarat. She possesses the fragrance and mettle of the soil. The treasure of her experiences has always been nurturing her. She is a teacher with emotional heart. An aspirant student is still alive in her. She always goes deep to the root to solve any problem. She bears a sentimental value of a teacher in her nature. Simplicity is her wealth. She is easily available to all. Any person who meets her experiences the smooth touch of her affection. Her minute observation always speaks for humanity. As a good public worker, her courtesy and care give richness to her approach towards public life. This book contains all the qualities of a **Handbook** for any active social worker.

This book could be a possible help, as a HANDBOOK, for a person who has devoted himself and engaged in social service. This Book by Anandiben brings to life the moments of those experiences of her public life which give a special recognition to her. The book is a tableau of her achievements & contributions to the society & the country. The incidents and events, as described in the book, show her extreme love, affection & devotion to serve the poor & the downtrodden class, women & the other weaker sections of the society. This innermost journey of her social and life can become a source of inspiration for many Teachers, Educationists and those in social service. After reading this Book, a Reader would be inclined to say—"I will remember this Book forever."